D1519371

BLOWN COVER

A Cuban Missile Crisis Novel

COPYRIGHT NOTICE
BLOWN COVER
BY PETER J. AZZOLE

ALSO BY PETER J. AZZOLE

HELL TO PAY
A Korean Conflict Novel
A Navy Pilot's Life-changing Adventure

ASSIGNMENT: BLETCHLEY
A WWII Novel of Navy Intelligence, Spies
(Tony Romella, U.S.N, WWII Assignments series Book 1)

ASSIGNMENT: LONDON
A WWII Novel of Naval Intelligence and Spies
(Tony Romella, U.S.N, WWII Assignments series Book 2)

ASSIGNMENT: NORWAY
A WWII Novel of Naval Intelligence and Spies
(Tony Romella, U.S.N, WWII Assignments series Book 3)

ASSIGNMENT: CASABLANCA
A WWII Novel of Naval Intelligence and Spies
(Tony Romella, U.S.N, WWII Assignments series Book 4)

ASSIGNMENT: PEENEMUNDE
A WWII Novel of Naval Intelligence and Spies
(Tony Romella, U.S.N, WWII Assignments series Book 5)

ASSIGNMENT: NORMANDY
A WWII Novel of Naval Intelligence and Spies
(Tony Romella, U.S.N, WWII Assignments series Book 6 of 6)

BLOWN COVER

A Cuban Missile Crisis Novel

Peter J. Azzole

DEDICATION

To the Cuban patriots who lost their lives in their
valiant struggles against the Castro regime

and

To Nancy,
for her patience with me
for the time I consume for writing

ACKNOWLEDGEMENTS

Beta readers Mrs. Nancy Azzole, Mr. Pedro Bello, Mrs. Sharon Friedheim, Mr. James Green, Mrs. Kathy Morrison, Mr. Harald Müller, Mrs. Linda Müller, Mrs. Veronica Sirotzky, and Mrs. Shirley Wang have my utmost gratitude for their detailed editorial reviews and insightful critiques of the draft manuscript.

Special and most sincere appreciation is due to Mrs. Laline Rojas for sharing her memories of life in Cuba and also to her daughter, Mrs. Veronica Sirotzky, for providing translations.

My gratitude is also extended to former Cuban Army Sergeant, Mr. Nelson Gonzales for discussing his experiences.

Thanks also go to Mr. David Fiehtner and Mr. "Gus" Gustafson for essential facts related to Naval Security Group history.

Last but not least is my appreciation for the support of the U.S. Naval Cryptologic Veterans Association.

Table of Contents

PREFACE

This story offers a fictional glimpse into the world of naval and national intelligence, and its challenges, within the framework of the events leading up to the Cuban Missile Crisis in 1962.

A Glossary at the end identifies the fictional characters and provides definitions for jargon, uncommon phrases, abbreviations, and other information.

Liberty has been taken in the creation of events and activities.

Times are given in local time.

Temperatures are Fahrenheit unless otherwise indicated.

Sources of declassified information are:

- https://www.nsa.gov/news-features/declassified-documents/cuban-missile-crisis/1963/
- https://www.jfklibrary.org
- https://www.cia.gov/readingroom/search/site/Cuban%20Missile%20Crisis
- https://stationhypo.com/2015/11/24/thirteen-days-the-naval-security-group-in-the-cuban-missile-crisis/
- https://www.allworldwars.com/Cuban-Missile-Crisis-CIA-Documents.html
- https://alphahistory.com/coldwar/joint-evaluation-soviet-missile-threat-cuba-1962/
- https://catalog.archives.gov/search?q=To%20the%20Brink:%20JFK%20and%20the%20Cuban%20Missile%20Crisis&f.oldScope=(descriptions%20or%20online)&SearchType=advanced

Peter J. Azzole

- https://www.history.com/news/cuban-missile-crisis-timeline-jfk-khrushchev
- https://historyinpieces.com/research/meetings-excomm-executive-committee-national-security-council
- https://en.wikipedia.org/wiki/Timeline_of_Cuban_history
- https://www.historycentral.com/JFK/Calendar/August1962.html
- https://www.historycentral.com/JFK/Calendar/September1962.html
- https://www.historycentral.com/JFK/Calendar/October1962.html
- https://www.thespacereview.com/article/4327/1

PROLOGUE

The Cuban Missile Crisis in 1962 was a near-war confrontation between the U.S. and the Soviet Union that lasted, from start to finish, only one month and four days—16 October–20 November 1962.

This crisis did not materialize overnight. Its infancy dates back two years to 1960 when suspicions arose that the Soviet Union was planning something untenable for the United States. The distance between the closest Cuban land and Key West was just short of a hundred miles of beautiful blue Florida Straits water. A significant Soviet military presence near the United States would be a clear and present danger.

Early concerns arose in 1960 when certain bits of intelligence gleaned from a multitude of sources were integrated. A Soviet arms export chief visited Havana. Then merchant ships from Soviet ports began bringing significant cargo loads of arms and related materials to Cuba. The Cuban government purchased Soviet helicopters. In concert, these and other puzzle pieces indicated that the Kremlin had a plan for a permanent and powerful military presence in Cuba.

Early in 1961, intelligence revealed that Cuban Air Force pilots were being trained in Czechoslovakia, and Cuban Air Force personnel were learning Russian. Soviet defensive radars were shipped to Cuba and installed strategically about the island. Throughout 1961 and 1962, a significant stream of Soviet cargo ships carried military arms and equipment from Soviet seaports in the Baltic. Upon arrival, many were purposely unloaded only during hours of darkness to avoid the ability of U.S. airborne or satellite reconnaissance to identify the types and amounts of their cargo.

During May and June of 1962, electronic intelligence discovered operational Soviet airborne intercept radars associated with Soviet MiG-17 and MiG-19 fighter aircraft. Human and electronic intelligence sources confirmed the presence of radars used with Soviet surface-to-air missiles. This was particularly alarming evidence of an operational threat to U.S. low-altitude reconnaissance flights that gathered valuable ground truth about the Soviet buildup. Thus, future reconnaissance flight paths were restricted and carefully planned.

The U.S. intelligence community regularly reported its findings to the National Security Council, among other consumers. The thirst for more insight into the Soviet plan resulted in the need for a more focused intelligence collection on Cuba.

In July 1962, the U.S. intelligence community and the National Security Council became highly concerned with mounting evidence that the Kremlin was establishing a significant offensive and potentially nuclear missile threat to the U.S. in Cuba. Secretary of Defense, Robert McNamara, ordered an increase in the Department's signal intelligence (SIGINT) resources and capability targeted at Cuba. The National Security Agency (NSA), the manager of Defense Department SIGINT resources, tasked the Naval Security Group (NAVSECGRU), the Navy's SIGINT organization, to augment its resources and prioritize its capability on Cuba. Other armed services were tasked likewise.

This is the environment that forms the backdrop of this novel.

BLOWN COVER

Peter J. Azzole

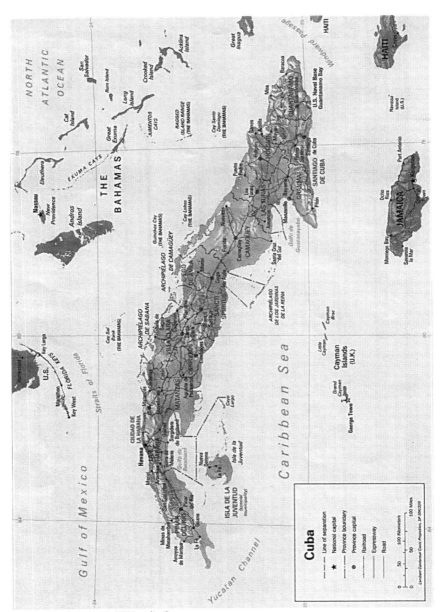

Cuba, Florida Keys, and surrounding area

1 – Excitement and Tears

Communications Technician (Interpretive) Petty Officer First Class (CT1) Salvador Conte, a 27-year-old Navy linguist, loved driving his pride and joy, a red 61 Chevy bubble-top Impala. But this was not a ride for fun; he was going to work. He parked outside the entrance of the 'elephant cage' antenna array that surrounded the Naval Security Group Activity Operations Building, located on Homestead Air Force Base, Florida.

US NavSecGru Command Display Photo

NSGA Homestead Antenna Array and Operations Building

He waited to turn off the engine to keep the air conditioner running while he listened to the rest of Freddy Cannon's *Palisades Park*. It was a scorcher of a July 1962 day. There would be no mercy from the sun. Once out of the Chevy, it would take mere seconds to swelter. Being called to report to the eve-watch an hour early without an explanation troubled him all the way from his apartment. He quick-stepped to the Operations Building entrance. The instantly cooling sensations of the building's powerful air conditioning system were more than welcome. He could almost hear his pores slamming shut as he walked down the hallway.

"Good afternoon, sir," said Salvador nervously, entering the minimally appointed sanctum of his Division Officer. A man in a gray pin-striped three-piece suit was already seated in front of the Lieutenant's desk. They traded polite nods.

Salvador sized the stranger up and thought, he's eyeing me like I'm prey. Must be crazy to wear a full suit here.

"Good afternoon, Conte. Have a seat," said the Lieutenant from behind his Navy standard-issue steel desk that showed evidence of a busy man with several works in progress. The Lieutenant's chair let out a multi-toned squeak as he leaned back and ran his fingers over his graying GI haircut. Salvador sat in the wooden chair a few feet from the civilian. "This is Mr. Jefferson. I called you in so he could ask you some questions before your watch begins. He is appropriately cleared, so you are free to answer in full detail."

"Aye, sir," Salvador said nervously. His mind was in high gear. I bet his ID says FBI. I can't think of anything I've done to stir up that hornet nest. I hope it's not about Angela.

"Alright, Conte," Jefferson began with emotionless and penetrating eyes. He crossed his legs and opened a notebook filled with hand-written notes.

Salvador's eyes dropped to the notebook. Its angle prevented him from seeing anything readable; he quickly looked away, feeling warmth in his cheeks from quickly building anxiety.

"I'm Marvin Jefferson, from a government agency. First, I'd like to ask if the nomenclature AN/G229P3B means anything to you?"

"No sir, never heard of it." Salvador took a deep breath.

"You didn't hesitate. Are you positive?"

"Affirmative sir," Salvador said with a shrug and thought to himself, he thinks I've seen or been near one. It doesn't even sound like a valid nomenclature. This should be a short interview.

Jefferson nodded, "OK. Let's move on. I've reviewed your personnel record, Conte, and would like to ask you some questions to fill in some details. It says you're fluent in Italian, Spanish, and Russian. How'd that happen?"

Calm down. Look him straight in the eye. Show him you're not intimidated. "Yes, sir. My father is Italian, my mother came from Cuba, and they each spoke to me mostly in those languages since I was a baby. They still do, and told me when I was a teenager that they felt it was important for me to know their native language. The Russian I learned when the Navy sent me to language school in Monterey."

"Did your mother understand the Italian?"

Why would he care about that? "Yes, sir. It became funny for me to hear them talk to each other in a mix of three languages. Which one they used seemed to depend on the subject."

"Was that confusing for you?"

He can't possibly give a rat's ass about all that. Must be his way of giving me easy stuff to break the ice. "Not at all."

"OK, now, about your request for SEAL training—why do you want to be a SEAL?"

Aha, that's it. Screening for SEAL school. "It's hard to explain, sir. But, I read in the Navy news about President Kennedy signing a bill that created SEALs last January. A TV program after that talked about their history and what they did. I guess it's my love of swimming, diving, and being in an elite group of Navy men that just inspired me. Not that I don't think CTs aren't an elite group, sir, because we are. I love what I'm doing. I sure do, and I'm good at it. SEALS just take service to the highest of highs."

Jefferson took copious notes as Salvador spoke. The Q&A went on for a half-hour, covering the details of his high school swim team accomplishments and his hobby of reef-diving in the Keys. Jefferson's questions then turned to Salvador's achievements on the base's intramural Rifle and Pistol Team. That led to a discussion of his hobby of collecting weapons from other countries and, more recently, pictures and details about the Cuban Army's weapons. Questioning then ventured into Salvador's knowledge of Cuban geography and its culture.

"Excellent, Conte," said Jefferson, "Let's talk about your technical training. Your record says you were initially trained as a Morse intercept operator at Imperial Beach, California."

Finally! This inquisition sounds like it's coming to an end. "Yes, sir, I graduated from basic CT R-branch School, but I was selected for language training in Monterey during my second week of advanced training."

"Did basic or advanced training include sending Morse?" asked Jefferson.

"No, sir, but I learned that on my own with a hand key and a battery-powered oscillator rig at home. Just as a kind of hobby. It's fun. I've been thinking about getting a ham radio license."

"Have you had the opportunity to intercept any Cuban or Russian Morse since you've been assigned to Homestead?"

"Affirmative, sir, but not much. When I reported aboard, my Chief had me spend a string of watches with the Morse Division. They put me side-saddle with one of the operators on a so-called easy circuit. Oh man, that was hard at first. Big difference between school Morse and live circuits. Especially without the benefit of the advanced course. But by the time the string of watches was over, I was holding my own."

Jefferson nodded, "Aside from raw translation work, have you done any analysis of transcripts or radio network analysis?"

What's this line of questions have to do with SEAL training? "Yes, sir, quite a bit of both at my last duty station and most of my time on watch here. If there's a backlog or someone's sick or on leave, I pinch hit with transcription and translation."

"OK. Good. Now, what does," he referred to his notes, "Miss Angela Mirabol know about your specialty in the Navy and your duties here?"

A shockwave of energy hit his stomach. Out of the blue, Angela? What the hell? OK, Sal, calm down. "Well, sir, she knows I'm a Communications Technician who does secure communications shift work. She knows I speak Italian and Spanish, thanks to mom and dad, but not about the Russian. That's about it, sir."

Jefferson's expression remained blank, keeping eye contact except to glance down as he took notes. "Alright! One more thing. Your performance evaluations frequently mention your unique ability to remember minute details. What can you tell me about that?"

Salvador laughed, "Yeah. I get that a lot. It's just something I've always been able to do. It's also why they usually put me in analysis. I don't even know I know stuff until the need for it arises, and there it is."

"Does it matter if you see, read, or hear things? Or can you remember no matter how you get it?"

"It doesn't seem to matter, sir."

"Does it depend on being a certain subject or anything?"

"I don't think it matters. Things, places, names, numbers, data, whatever."

"Oh, I forgot to ask you earlier when we talked about your gun collection. Which of the Cuban military small arms is your favorite?"

Wow! This guy asks some damn off-the-wall stuff. "Oh, I think they are using mostly U.S. and Russian weapons. But as far as a weapon I'd like to have in the collection I keep at dad's house, it would be the Spanish M98Mauser. I won't bore you with my reasons."

Jefferson looked him straight in the eye and asked, "Conte, which government agency did I say I represented?"

"You didn't say, sir. You only said that you were from a government agency."

"And what was the nomenclature I asked you about?"

"AN/G229P3B, sir," Salvador replied without hesitation.

"I guess you do have a good memory. Thank you very much, Conte," said Jefferson, showing a smile for the first time. He closed his notebook and returned a government-issue pen to his inside jacket pocket. "He's all yours, Lieutenant, thank you. I can find my way out." He stood, shook their hands, and departed.

"What's this all about, sir?" asked Salvador.

"It's about your response to the call from Security Group Headquarters for specific linguist volunteers a couple weeks ago. Well, it looks like you're on the shortlist."

"Oh, yes, the special assignment with the meaningless description," Salvador said with a chuckle. "I must have been nuts to volunteer for something in the blind. Anyway, since I figured he was FBI, I didn't think it was about that. So, do you have more info on this thing now, sir?"

"You know as much as I do, Conte."

A few days later, Salvador's day watch was interrupted by another visit to his Division Officer.

"Have a seat, Conte. "Things have moved surprisingly fast in DC. You've been selected for that assignment, providing you remain interested."

Salvador felt his face flush, and anticipation skyrocket.

Before he could speak, the Lieutenant continued. "It's a mission you must consider carefully before volunteering." He handed Salvador a one-page document marked TOP SECRET in red at the top and bottom of the page. "That's a description of the mission for you to read before you make a commitment."

The heading of the document was *'Joint CIA/NAVSECGRU Operation Cymbal Beat Volunteer Summary.'* Salvador read the text carefully. The final paragraph's last sentence quickened his heart rate, and a rush of adrenalin sent tingles through his body. *"Thus, you will be covertly inserted by the Navy into an area of Cuba that will likely yield the required intelligence, and where CIA sources will provide cover..."* He finished reading, looked up, and handed the page back to the Lieutenant with a slightly trembling hand.

"I know this is a shock, but before you say anything, Conte, there's no more to know about this until you formally sign up for it. But I want to emphasize that you can decline without any fear of negatively impacting your next evaluation or career. You should know that you were selected from a list of 11 Army, Navy, and Air Force volunteers."

"I don't know what to say, sir."

"Don't say anything, Conte. Not until you've given this a lot of thought. I'll need your answer by noon tomorrow."

After a deep halting breath, Salvador realized his life was about to take a drastic turn. After his mind spun for a few moments, he thought, I must be crazy, but I have to do this. He swallowed hard; "Sir, I don't need any more time to think about it. I definitely volunteer."

The Lieutenant grinned, "I'm not surprised. That being the case, I have a volunteer document for you to sign. You will travel to DC and perform your duties there in civilian clothes. Go to Admin at 0900 tomorrow to pick up your orders and travel vouchers, then…" he continued with his instructions to Salvador.

After two hectic and wildly exciting weeks in Washington, DC, Salvador shook the hands of Agent Marvin Jefferson and Captain Daniel Patterson before getting out of the government staff car at Washington National Airport.

"Fair winds and following seas, Conte," said Patterson.

"Thank you, Captain. I hope that will be the case."

"Good luck, Salvador," said Jefferson. "A lot of people will be looking out for you."

"Thank you, sir. I'll need those people and all the luck I can get."

Sitting at the gate, waiting to board his flight to Miami, Salvador thought back over the two-week whirlwind of briefings, training, and planning meetings.

At CIA HQ in Langley, he was given carefully screened intelligence on the Soviet buildup and information about his destination area in Cuba. Additionally, he received a minimum of details about Soviet anti-ship, anti-air, and ballistic missile systems. The week at Langley ended with hand-to-hand combat, radio reporting procedures, and pertinent tradecraft.

Then it was on to Naval Security Group HQ at Nebraska Avenue in Washington, DC, also known by its Navy organizational code, OP-20-G.

"Your first time at headquarters?" asked Captain Patterson as they shook hands.

"Yes, sir. I'm glad you sent that seaman to escort me. I would have gotten lost."

"Have a seat. Welcome to G50, Operations. We have a full two days lined up for you. We're going to give you only what you need to know to do this mission, just like they did at Langley. We have to consider the worst-case scenario. You understand that."

"Yes, sir, I do. Let's hope it doesn't come to that."

"The odds are very low, but they are not zero. You were on top of the list of volunteers for this mission because you lacked involvement in highly sensitive programs thus far in your career. It also helped that you are single, have extensive linguistic proficiencies, and a unique combination of skills."

"I wondered about that. It makes sense."

"Well, I'm glad you volunteered. The Navy has a keen interest in this mission, namely, the Soviet anti-ship missile threat. Not that the national intelligence interest isn't important, but having a Navy man on this mission is important to us."

"Roger that, sir."

"Alright, I just wanted to talk to you first before sending you off to the analysts and weather-guessers. My yeoman will take you to your next stop."

Salvador spent the rest of the day with the Operations Department analysts, learning all the details of the Navy's interests in this mission. Time was allotted the following day to huddle with a small team of highly cleared Navy weather forecasters, learning the expected weather, tides, and ocean currents for Salvador's destination waters and beach.

After that, there were briefings at the National Security Agency (NSA) Fort George G. Meade, Maryland. Soviet analysts gave him certain details, idiosyncrasies, and priorities of the voice communications circuits that were Salvador's intercept targets.

As he sat, waiting impatiently for the boarding announcement, it struck him that Salvador Conte, born and raised in south Jersey, with only high school education, was now on a Top Secret and clearly dangerous joint operation for the CIA and OP-20-G. There were times when it all seemed like a novel or movie. But reality slammed home; it was real, very real. It made him, at once, anxious, nervous, excited, and proud.

He could barely control his excitement when he boarded the PanAm flight to Miami International Airport. He looked forward to the drive to his apartment in Homestead, Florida, where the love of his life waited anxiously but was unaware of the news he was bringing. There was so little he could share with her, which would be difficult. It would be a bittersweet return with a potentially undesired outcome. *If she can handle this, she can handle the rest of my Navy career. She's tough. She'll handle it. I hope.*

During the flight to Miami, he found it difficult to concentrate. He wanted to read an article in a magazine he found in the seatback pouch in front of him. It was about increasing the muscle power of a car's engine in the July issue of Popular Science. But visions of Angela kept interrupting his focus. He reminisced how it was practically a case of love at first sight when they met one weekend in a Key Largo, Florida bar. The one where the locals alleged that Bogie and Bacall filmed a scene in the movie *Key Largo* some 15 years before that. Original film posters on the walls and the assurances of the bartender validated the assertion. He recalled how she captured his attention when she came into the bar with a girlfriend. Although he had no memory of what her friend was wearing, he had a vivid memory of her blue and white print sundress accentuating her narrow waist. She was a few inches shorter than his 5'11". Her long, lusciously thick brown hair seemed to float with her every move. Vibrant red lipstick attracted his eyes as he watched her walk to the bar and sit just two stools from him. He could not resist talking to her.

"Can I buy you two ladies a drink?" he said before the bartender had a chance to get their order.

Angela turned and made eye contact with Salvador and smiled. "You can buy me one," she said with a voice that melted his heart. "Captain Morgan and Coke, thank you, sir."

"Thank you, but I'll wait for my date," said her friend. "He'll be here soon."

"On my tab," he said, nodding to the bartender. Turning back to Angela, "I'm Salvador! Call me Sal." Pointing to the stool beside her, he asked, "May I?"

She flashed a bright-eyed sweet smile, giving the stool beside her a pat, "Hello, Sal. I'm Angela. You can call me Ang. Nice to meet you."

He couldn't stop smiling at her. "Same here. So, Angela, Ang, would you like to dance?"

"Let's talk and enjoy our drinks a bit. Then, if you're a good boy, we'll dance," she said playfully.

They talked through two rounds of drinks about their Cuban roots and families. Learning that they both lived and worked in Homestead put broad smiles on their faces. They already knew they wanted to see more of each other. Their fate had been set.

"Alright, Sal," she said as the jukebox began playing *Roses Are Red,* "let's dance."

When they came into the close hold for the slow dance, he said, "Oh, Ang, what is that heavenly perfume?"

She giggled, "Nothing fancy. It's just Avon, one called Occur!"

"It might not be fancy, but it's intoxicating to me."

"That's the idea, Sal," she said with a chuckle.

"Mission accomplished, Ang," he said, grinning.

They shared a bowl of bar snacks, nursed two more Captain and Cokes, and danced Friday night away, learning more about each other's lives and aspirations. The chemistry between them was palpable. They spent the remainder of that Key Largo weekend together. Two magnets were fatefully brought together. She moved in with him two months later.

The reverie of that magical Key Largo weekend faded from his mind. In their seven months together, aside from this trip to DC, they were never apart for more than one of his watches. That was going to change, and soon. How she'd react to his news had been worrisome from when he deplaned in Miami to now, as he parked outside his apartment. Before getting out of the car, he paused, thinking, I hope this goes well. I think it will. I wish I knew for sure.

Angela Mirabol met Salvador at their apartment door in a filmy, skimpy purple negligee he had never seen. The girls in the salon where she worked as a hairdresser had done their best to make her look incredible. Oh my God, she's beautiful. How in hell can I tell her what's in store.

"Drop those bags, sailor," she said in a sultry voice he hadn't heard before. He shut and locked the door. As his bags hit the floor, she stood back and turned slowly, grinning.

He gazed from her flowing hair, and stunning negligee, to her bare feet.

"You like?" she asked devilishly when his eyes returned to hers.

"Hell yeah!" he exclaimed with a wink, then pulled her into his arms.

After they hugged and kissed, she took his hand and led him to the bedroom, where they made passionate love until they were exhausted. They whispered lovingly to each other in the afterglow, their arms and legs tangled, hugging and kissing tenderly. They quietly savored being back together.

"There are times when silence is a poignant part of the music," he said, recalling a passage from a novel.

"Yes, Sal. Not the first time you said that, but very true."

"Getting hungry, Chica?" he asked with a broad smile, combing his fingers through the length of her soft fine hair that had a perfume-like aroma of tropical fruit conditioner.

"You just had dinner, Sal," Angela said with a wink. Then raising up on an elbow, chuckling softly, she cooed, "Ready for dessert?"

Later, while they lay spooned in a tight hug, ravished again to exhaustion, his mind nudged him to an unwelcome reality. I need to find that right situation and words to tell her that I'm leaving in two days. Oh, God, I need some help here.

She turned and ran a finger across his lips slowly, "I'll go take a quick shower while you get your bags unpacked. Put your laundry in the basket by the washing machine. There's a load of towels about to finish now. I'll take care of all your stuff tomorrow."

"OK, chica," he said, rolling out of bed. He picked up his boxers and t-shirt, tossed them in the basket, and went to get his bags sitting by the door.

Salvador returned from the shower in fresh white boxers. The washing machine was making its usual squeaks and groans, a window air-conditioner was laboring with a rhythmic drone, and a ceiling fan hummed softly over the couch. The TV displayed the Roy Rogers and Dale Evans Show, but the volume was turned down very low. Angela was waiting with a smile on the sofa in summer pajamas.

He sat down, put his arm around her, and tugged her close. "I love you, Ang."

She turned her head, flashed a loving smile, and kissed him. "I love and adore you, Sal." She reached to the side table and handed him a tall cold glass emblazoned with etchings of palm trees topped with a slice of lime.

"Oh, I've been craving a rum and Coke! Gracias!"

"Our favorite drink. To us!"

"To us!" he said, touching his glass to hers.

"I hope you have some days off after all that," she said with cheery optimism.

Seeing her facial expression change meant that she recognized his hesitance to confirm her hopes. He wished he already had three or ten of these drinks. "I have to leave again in two days at the crack of dawn." Damn it, where'd those words come from. I didn't mean for it to come out like that.

When those mind-numbing words stopped echoing in her ears, she managed to say with a quiet voice and tears forming, "Oh my God, Sal. Where are you going, and for how long?"

"Back to DC for more temporary duty."

"You didn't say how long."

Salvador took a deep breath, "I really don't know; it could be, uh, weeks, maybe months."

"Oh! Well then, I'll take some vacation days to come up and stay for a long weekend now and then," she said with cautious optimism. "You can show me around DC. I've always wanted to see the White House."

"Uh, no, Ang, I'll be bunking in enlisted quarters. That won't be possible."

Angela's expression went quickly to a puzzled look with wet eyes, "Well, I'm sure hotels are too expensive in DC. You'll call me every night then?"

Salvador felt a tennis ball lodge in his throat. "Um, no, Ang, I won't be allowed to make any calls. It's a security thing."

She snuggled against him, "What's going on, Sal?"

"It's a high security project, Ang. When it's over, I'll be back, and things will be back to normal."

"Are you really going to Washington?"

"You'll just have to accept my explanation, Chica." He wiped mascara-tinted tears from her cheeks with his fingers. "It's just how it is with my job, sweetheart."

2 – Point Orange

Salvador stepped onto the gangplank of a diesel-powered submarine at Mayport Naval Station, Jacksonville, Florida. As he walked across, treads creaking under his shoes, his mind flashed back momentarily to Angela's river of tears and almost painfully tight hug that morning. He realized it would be necessary for his safety to muster the discipline, as best he could, to push personal emotions well into his core for the rest of this mission.

Seamen on deck were looking at him incredulously. A man with two seabags, driven to the dock in a Navy staff car, reporting aboard in dungarees, was a glaring oddity. A Lieutenant, wearing an OOD (Officer of the Deck) armband, came to the gangplank and waited.

Salvador saluted the OOD, "Permission to come aboard, sir. Petty Officer First Class Conte reporting for duty, sir." He offered his sealed orders envelope to the OOD

The Lieutenant returned the salute, "Permission granted. Go below and find the Chief of the Boat. He'll take you to the skipper. Give those orders to him personally."

"Oh, he's definitely a spook," whispered a Petty Officer Second Class to a nearby Seaman. "At least he's got a regulation haircut. Show him how to get below and where to go."

Salvador heard the remark, smiled internally, and followed the seaman into the bowels of the boat. As soon as his feet hit the deck at the bottom of the ladder, the smells of a submarine's interior gave his sense of smell a new experience. The further he went toward the Captain's cabin, the stronger the complex odor mixture became of diesel fuel, motor oil, a gymnasium locker room, and others he couldn't identify.

The timeline in the sealed orders for Operation Cymbal Beat—the delivery of a Navy agent to Cuba—was followed precisely. The submarine ran for two days at full speed on the surface from Mayport to a waypoint 10 miles southeast of Key West, Florida. Upon arrival at that waypoint, with the sun nearing the horizon, a course change to the southwest was executed. As the sun sank into the horizon, creating a magnificent red-tinted sky, the Captain ordered a deep dive to avoid detection by Soviet or Cuban ships and aircraft and proceeded at a depth of 180 feet. That depth put them below an ocean temperature thermocline that would inhibit detection from surface-ship sonars. Speed was calculated to arrive at a navigation point designated as Orange at the time specified in the Cymbal Beat orders. Point Orange was 3.1 miles directly off a beach located 25 miles east of Havana in international waters.

Salvador was sitting in the sub's small mess deck, nursing a mug of strong, hot Navy coffee, waiting for the call to get ready to swim. As usual, those coming through the mess deck ignored him as though he had a mysterious disease. That was fine with Salvador; there wouldn't be any questions he couldn't answer. While four men played poker on the table next to him, memories of Angela wandered through his mind, mingling with visualizations of the next portion of the operation.

Suddenly the Chief of the Boat, known as the COB, stepped into the hatch of the mess deck and pointed at Salvador. "Lay-to aft torpedo and suit up."

He downed the rest of the coffee and thought, this is the day. Man, oh man, August 12, 1962. I'll remember this date for the rest of my life—hopefully, it will be a long one.

Salvador hurried aft in the ubiquitous red glow of the night-routine lighting, which preserved everyone's night vision. The Control Room was packed with a plotting table, officers, men, pipes, valves, levers, and panel lights. Several pairs of eyes watched him pass through; he was the sole reason they were here, and they would be on their way back to port when he was gone.

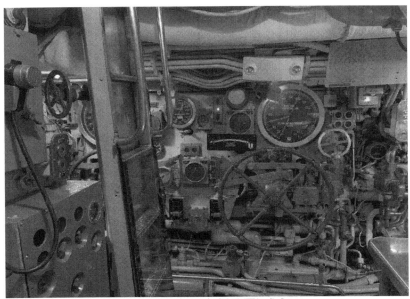

Diesel submarine control room in normal light

The walk aft became easier as the bow raised a few degrees, making it a downhill walk to the torpedo room as the boat rose to the surface. As he moved along, the hull creaked now and then from decreasing external water pressure. He stepped through the aft torpedo room hatch and took off his shoes, socks, and dungarees, leaving him barefoot, wearing just swim trunks, a watch on the left hand, and a wrist compass on the other. He turned to an empty section of a torpedo skid where he had earlier laid out underwater breathing apparatus and other gear he'd be taking. First on was the wet suit. Then, piece by piece, he donned other items: a combat knife to the lower leg, wading shoes, a weight belt with a flashlight attached, an air tank, which he checked for 100% air

4

before securing it to his back, a regulator, and last, a face mask and snorkel, which he pulled up onto his forehead. He checked the sealed rubber bag he would tow on a lanyard. It contained Cuban civilian clothing and other critical items. Salvador nodded to the Chief of the Boat.

"Control, COB, aft torpedo, swimmer ready!"

"Roger, COB. ETA Point Orange 22 minutes."

Salvador checked his watch. Good, right on time, 18 minutes ahead of 0030. God, help me through this. I love you, Angela. He felt a small adrenalin release. In less than a half-hour, he'd be swimming toward a Cuban beach, separated from this safe environment.

The relatively quiet electric motor turning the propeller hummed in Salvador's ears. The boat crept toward its destination, rising to periscope depth below a relatively calm surface.

He sat cross-legged on the cold steel deck, eyes closed, mentally rehearsing the plan for swimming ashore and all possible situations and options. Let's hope this goes OK. A shiver rippled through his core. Eyes closed, he let visions of his sugar plum, Angela, dance in his head briefly.

The hum of the motors quit, and the boat went silent, jolting him back to reality. They were at Point Orange, at periscope depth, dead in the water, and in radio silence. Crewmen were quietly assessing the possible existence of air, surface, or subsurface threats by periscope, passive radar, and sonar. M-minute of the operation plan seemed an eternity away.

The intercom broke the silence, "Aft torpedo, Control, surfacing two minutes." Just then, the diesel engines came to life. The boat's snorkel mast had been raised above the sea to begin recharging the batteries and exchanging the air in the boat that had gotten starved of oxygen and somewhat foul.

The smell of fresh air flowing into the compartments brought to mind how acclimated one becomes to air changed from humans occupying a closed area.

Salvador made final checks of his belts, straps, and gear. His heart began to pound as additional adrenalin coursed through his arteries, making his mouth dry and his skin tickle. Crewmen were rigging the ladder to the deck hatch. He closed his eyes and said a mental prayer.

5

Diesel submarine aft torpedo room

Suddenly, the intercom announced Battle Stations. The Ooga horn blared, followed by the sounds of ballast tanks blowing water out and filling with air to increase buoyancy.

Smiling, he thought, this is it! Time for a little swim. He slipped an arm through the straps of the swim fins to free his hand, grabbed his rubber gear bag, and followed crewmen up the ladder and onto the wet deck.

The scant sliver of the moon provided only enough light to see outlines of two men securing a rope to help Salvador carefully descend the short distance over the rounded side of the sub's stern into the dark tepid sea. A light balmy breeze lapped Florida Strait waters against the hull, making a pleasant rhythmic splashing sound. Salty droplets in the air could be smelled and tasted. I'll soon find out if all the snorkeling and diving in Key Largo, swimming against those tides, was enough to get me through this.

A pat on his back and a thumbs-up from a man on deck meant all was ready for him. Salvador sat down, put on his flippers, secured his snorkel and face mask, took a quick look at the luminous hands of his watch, and repelled over the side into a bathtub that stretched three miles to the other end. The arduous swim on the surface began with a quick check of the softly glowing readings of the compass on his wrist to get his bearings. The eerie sound behind him of the sub's deck hatch shutting and ballast tanks blowing air to dive was a reality check.

Salvador stopped swimming when the expected landmark lights ashore came into view. He referred to his compass and whispered into the balmy, humid air, "Now that's good news. I'm close to a perfect track."

Forecasts for the prevailing ocean currents provided by the Aerographer's Mates at OP-20-G appeared to be accurate, based on his relative position from the landmarks.

Just then, he detected the distant but unnerving sounds of a Cuban shore patrol boat. A chill raced through his gut when its searchlight scanned through his location. They can't see me at this distance. He looked at his watch. At least I know they are on the expected schedule. So far, so good.

The information he received from analysts on patrol boats and their schedules for this area was confirmed. He smiled and put the snorkel back in his mouth. If their schedule holds, I won't need to use the air in my tank, or not often, anyway. The air tank was his counter to patrol craft that would get within their spotlights' visual range, allowing him to submerge for the time needed to avoid detection.

Nearly two hours into the laborious swim, it was clear to Salvador that the pace he set was achieving the speed goal. It wasn't easy, with the tank on his back and a bag in tow. It took brute force discipline to maintain a rhythm of stroking, kicking, and deep breathing while ignoring increasing muscle burn. He occupied his mind by rehearsing the final procedures when nearing shore and making contact with a man named Tomas.

About a mile from the beach, a Cuban patrol craft came into view on a course that would pass from left to right, parallel to the coast. Damn it, he's gonna get too close. He pulled the regulator to his mouth and ducked ten feet under while maintaining slow progress toward the beach. When waning propeller sounds indicated that the patrol craft had passed, he resumed his swim on the surface. The Cuban coastal patrol schedule he memorized suggested the remainder of the swim to the beach was theoretically safe. Once ashore, it would be another story. A host of unknowns awaited there.

Pausing 200 yards from the shoreline, Salvador checked his watch and scanned the scarcely discernable outline of the beach area. A short red flashlight signal from Tomas, a CIA contact, was expected to begin in seven minutes. Then it would be repeated every two minutes for one hour. Failing to make contact would force the execution of abort-option 1, which wasn't the least bit desirable. That option was to swim back three miles and get close enough to the submarine for them to see his flashlight signals before their contingency waiting period expired.

The time spent treading water allowed precious time to rest his aching muscles and catch his breath. There it was! A red flashlight blinked off to the right, sending the prearranged Morse equivalent for the letter D. Salvador flashed his response—the letter U. The counter-reply from shore, S, was confirmation that his reply had been seen. He began swimming toward shore. At 100 yards from the beach, Salvador took off his underwater breathing gear, released all the air from the tank, tied all the gear together with the lanyard used to tow the bag, and let it free to sink with the weight belt to the bottom. Combat knife now strapped to his thigh, and the rubber bag worn as a backpack, he swam the remainder of the way to shore.

"Sergio?" the man said softly, standing near the water's edge.

Salvador waded toward him, "Tomas?" I sure hope this guy can be trusted.

"Yes, yes. How are your legs after that swim?"

"Burning, but I'm OK." Salvador trudged the last few yards to dry land. There was a sense of relief when he felt and heard dry sand crunch under his shoes. He kneeled briefly to catch his breath and relieve his legs. He got back up in a few moments, and they shook hands firmly.

"Get to the tall shrubs to change," said Tomas. "No more English from here on!"

A tightly rolled bath towel in the rubber bag was a blessing. Salvador dried off and changed into the street clothes packed in the bag. They used their hands to dig a hole to bury the towel and swim trunks and covered the hole carefully with sand. The backpack now contained only the bound one-time-pad pages Salvador would use to encrypt messages sent to the CIA at Langley and two sets of underwear.

Tomas put his hand on Sergio's shoulder, "We have more than two miles to walk, Sergio, and it is mostly off-road. They should have given you boots, not shoes. Let me know if you need to rest a bit now and then. But we need to get to my house before sunlight."

"We will get going now. I'll be fine," said Sergio, powered with a continuing flow of adrenalin from the inherent insecurities of being in the open on Cuban soil.

"We should have enough time. The first hint of light will come about five-thirty. Stay close."

Sergio kept up with the quick pace set by Tomas, whose faint outline was that of a man several inches shorter and slim. Trailing close behind Tomas, he realized that, not many days from now, he, too, would smell strong from not having the luxury of deodorant.

Their meandering route kept them away from roads where anyone, especially Cuban military or police, might be encountered this time of night. Traveling through fields, undeveloped areas of pesky brush, dirt roads, and footpaths led to the outskirts of a small village two miles southwest of Santa Cruz.

They passed through a wooden gate in a rock wall and entered the backyard of a silhouetted two-story building. "Be careful not to trample the vegetables," said Tomas, navigating between the rows. "My home, Sergio."

"Thank God," said Salvador, feeling totally spent.

Tomas opened the back door of the building slowly to minimize the noise from old hinges, held it for Sergio to pass through, closed it just as slowly, locked it, and turned on a red-lens flashlight. "This is my auto repair shop. I live in the adjoining building through that door on the other side of the bay. You will be living up in the garage attic. Follow me."

The light gave Sergio his first sight of his host's face. It was expressionless. His thick curly hair was a very dark brown or black in the red light.

The open bay of the garage had space for two cars, one with a hand-powered lift. The walls were bare corrugated steel, showing some rust. They walked past the side of an old Chevy and up a steep, straight flight of metal stairs against the wall to an enclosed attic room.

Tomas pointed his flashlight at the light switch at the top of the stairs just outside a closed door. "I removed the bulb from the ceiling light in the room, so this doesn't work. I don't want external evidence of activity up here after dark. As far as anyone knows, it's a storage area."

"Good idea," said Salvador.

"Use the table lamp on the desk at the other end of the room. It's only a 25-watt bulb, but it's sufficient for you to work and see what you are doing in the rest of the room. Electricity use is monitored, so be sure to use it only when necessary." He turned the doorknob, pushed open the door, and stepped into the room. "Take a look around, Sergio. It's not much, but it is not too bad."

Salvador heard the smile in Tomas' voice. He stepped into the unlit 8'x10' room and scanned the red beam of his own flashlight around.

Cigarette and cigar smoke odors lingered. The walls up here were also bare rusty corrugated steel. A low ceiling of unfinished wallboard was crudely mounted a few inches above his head. An unmade cot was on one end of the room, with an unfished wood side table and a rug. There were folded linens on the mattress. A small round wooden table and two chairs were in the middle of the room. A smile formed on his face when he trained the light to the far end of the room, where he saw a stool by a 4'x6' table with radios, headphones, a stack of paper, and pencils.

"Those radios and things on the table are just as they were left by the last man. Be sure to turn off the radios when you're done.

"I understand, Tomas. Use the least amount of electricity."

"Yes. Also, about security. It might be obvious, Sergio, but I'll say this anyway. Theoretically, the biggest threat to you is getting discovered up here. If that happens, we'll all be in prison, or worse. Keep that in mind with everything you do."

"Understood, Tomas."

"Good. In that line of thought, keep the window curtains closed during the day and use the black curtain at night. Don't be tempted to look out the window. Oh, and in the drawer of the side table by the cot, there is a Browning pistol with a silencer and some ammo. Take it out, load it, and always keep it with you or within reach. Before I forget to ask you, what last name are you using?"

"Lopez. What's yours?"

"You can tell me your cover story after you've gotten some sleep. Tomas Alvarez is my real name, and don't be afraid to use it. The government and everyone around here knows me by that name. Alright, Mr. Lopez, here's how our daily routine will go. My wife makes three servings for each meal, but I'll bring yours up here. She doesn't want anything to do with you. She wasn't happy having somebody up here before and likes it even less now with the Soviets coming into the island by the hundreds.

"I guess I understand why she feels that way."

"She wishes I would stop what I'm doing too, but she knows it's the right thing for our country."

"I'm curious, Tomas, how were you able to keep your garage after the Castro government declared ownership of businesses?"

"I was careful to remain quiet about the government takeover and

11

what they've done. The local authorities want to be able to have their cars repaired, so they are lenient about the size of my vegetable garden and get me parts and materials. I know they are watching, though. Always watching. So I am cautious about what I do."

"I suppose I'm in the same boat as you are with your wife. If my girlfriend knew what I was doing, she'd be worried sick and would probably think I was crazy. About security, rest assured, I'll be even more careful than you."

Tomas nodded, "Good. I'll wake you when breakfast is ready later this morning. I'm sure you'll be hungry, but don't expect much. After that, I'll leave your breakfast inside the door if you're asleep. Also, it's none of my business when you sleep, what you do, or when you do it. Keep your door closed. When I come up to talk or bring meals, I'll knock and wait for a response before entering. Anything but a two-two knock will mean grab the pistol and prepare to defend yourself. You can always tell me to come back later, too."

"Good, Tomas. Have you ever had anyone get curious about the attic?"

"Not for a couple years. Let's hope it stays that way."

"Sounds like a good plan for food and security. How about my laundry?"

"There's a laundry bag among the things on the cot. We'll take care of that too. Sergio, make sure you don't leave this garage for any reason. Do you understand?"

Salvador nodded, "Yes. I do. A hermit's life with bare necessities was how they explained it to me. How about toilet, sink, and shower?"

"Those are downstairs, below this room, next to my office. I know they monitor water use, so make your showers really fast and only once a week. Also, no flushing except for poop. No shaving either."

"I understand, Tomas," Salvador said with a chuckle.

"Also, there is a military airport two kilometers to the northwest. We're close to the path planes use when taking off from one of the runways. It can get noisy when they are training."

Salvador nodded, "Is it the Cuban air force there, or have the Soviets moved in too?"

"They're both over there now."

"I have more questions, but I'm beat; I can barely keep my eyes open.

I need to sleep. I'll figure out what I have up here after breakfast."

"Good. Sleep well. I'll be waking you in about four hours."

Four hours, oh my God, I need ten. Salvador took off his backpack and put it on the floor by the bed. He moved the things lying on the cot to the top of the side table and opened the drawer for quick access to the pistol. His mind began to wander as he stretched out, still in his street clothes, on the bare, musty-smelling, perspiration-stained mattress. This feels like heaven. Who was living up here before, and why aren't they still here? I wish he hadn't been a smoker.

There were a lot of questions for Tomas, but they would have to wait until tomorrow. Shortly after taking a deep breath, his exhausted and adrenalin-ravaged body drifted quickly into a deep sleep.

3 – Overalls and Skivvies

Two knocks, followed by two knocks, woke Salvador. Daylight was visible at the edges of the curtains above the cot. A rooster crowed, and chickens clucked in the distance. "Come on in. I'm starving. But first, I need to use the head."

"It's safe to go down now, but make it quick," said Tomas. "I'll leave this on the table for you."

"OK, could you come back up in half an hour?" asked Salvador as he reached up to tie the black curtain material aside to allow more sunlight.

Salvador's stomach growled as he put his spoon down in an empty bowl. They told me there would be food rationing, but damn, that breakfast left me hungry. Breakfast had been a bowl of rice and beans, made incredibly tasty by merely adding some sugar water. The slice of buttered Cuban bread and a demitasse cup of strong, sweet café Cubano left him wanting more of that too. It wasn't sating his hunger after the extensive energy he burned to get here, but he was grateful. He heard chickens clucking as they roamed the garden in the backyard. Smiling, he thought, oh, that's music to my ears. Maybe I'll get some fresh eggs and hopefully some vegetables.

It was time to go to the table at the other end of the room to check the radio equipment. There were U.S.-made UHF and VHF band receivers and an HF band (shortwave) transceiver. "Perfect," he whispered to himself. An antenna wire ran up the back wall and through a small hole in the ceiling. He applied power briefly to all the radio units, one after the other, smiling as they energized. Their lighted dials and meters showed they were working normally.

Tomas knocked on the door and asked, "Everything good?"

Salvador got off the stool and replied, "Seems to be. Come in."

A present for me?" Salvador asked with a smile, pointing at what Tomas was carrying.

"An early Christmas present," Tomas said with a chuckle. "Hide those civilian clothes. It gets so hot up here that you'll want to work in your underwear. But put on these overalls when you go downstairs. I wore them yesterday to work on cars to give them some grease smears and stains. Also, leave that watch up here. That thing will create more questions than you want. If someone comes in while you're down there, you need to look and act like my mechanic."

Salvador grinned, "Alright. Good idea! I've worked on cars a lot, so I can play that part. But you are shorter than me. Will these fit?"

Tomas laughed, "Oh, they don't fit me, but I wore them anyway, just to get them dirty. I had an assistant who wore them. He's been gone for about a year and a half now. He got married and quit to work with his father-in-law in a Central, a cane processing plant. I have another pair of these if you need a change, but unless you shit yourself, they should last you." They both had a good laugh. "Also, Sergio, if anyone comes in while you're downstairs, don't come back up here while they are in the shop."

"Of course, Tomas."

"The more Soviets that come into this country, the tighter Castro's security is getting. We need to be really careful. Something big seems to be going on, and I haven't figured out what it is yet. I just report what I see and hear and wait for instructions."

"I don't do any reporting for you, do I?" asked Salvador.

"Oh, no, I have my own means. I just house and feed you. Otherwise, we're completely independent."

"I'm really glad you're so careful," Salvador said, realizing Tomas' activities and reporting could jeopardize both. "By the way, is an electric fan out of the question?"

"Yes, sorry, we don't have one either. We just don't wear much and sleep naked."

"Alright. First, I'm curious about what happened to the guy that was up here before? They told me what equipment I would find but nothing else."

"All I know is that he left when they closed the U.S. Embassy in Havana last year. He used to go out at night sometimes, but what he was doing, I had no idea and didn't want to know. Same with you. I'm just providing you food and a place to work to help bring down Castro and his communist government one day. There are a lot of us all over this island that are counting on the United States. Things just seem to get worse by the day, and we don't think this influx of Soviets will be any help. One question for you. Do you have an escape plan that I need to know about?"

I wasn't expecting him to ask me about that. Let's hope the Cuban State Security hasn't gotten to him. "All I know, Tomas, is that they will provide instructions when it is time." I hope that satisfies him for now. I don't want to discuss my contingencies unless it's critical.

Tomas shook his head, "I wouldn't be happy with that. If you should need any help, just ask."

"Thank you, I appreciate your help. By the way, Tomas, I'll need a five-gallon can or a big crock to burn papers. A screen to cover it would be good, to keep burning ashes from flying out. Also, I'll need matches."

"I'll try and come up with something in the next day or two."

Tomas was working on the Chevy in the garage bay. Salvador was at the radio table with headphones on and receivers energized. A quick scan across the UHF and VHF bands found voice circuits with varied strengths. Some of them were Cuban, and some were Russian. His doubts about the efficiency of the yet unseen antenna above the ceiling were put aside. Turning to the HF band transceiver, he found that the Morse marker of the shortwave network he would use to communicate was loud and clear on two frequencies of the five they had him memorize. During the course of 24 hours, usable frequencies would change, but those he had would ensure at least one would suffice. Next, he connected the HF band transmitter output to the dummy load used for safely testing off-air and smiled at the results. Hot damn, I'm operational.

Salvador encrypted a brief status message. It was a two-word code phrase he memorized at CIA Headquarters, Langley, to signify that he arrived safely, that he was with the CIA contact, and that all equipment was operational.

Salvador energized the transceiver and tuned it to the best frequency for the CIA Morse circuit. Adrenalin was now raging through his body. The reality that he was about to make his first radio transmission in the open was exciting, but not in a good way. Despite the intelligence briefs he received that there was no evidence of mobile direction-finding equipment in Cuba, it was impossible not to worry about transmitting and getting discovered. The Soviets would surely establish a radio intercept station in Cuba at some point. Following that, they'd establish a direction-finding (DF) capability as well, including mobile DF vans. Those vans would be able to locate him quickly. He had to keep faith that Washington would let him know if the Soviets developed such a capability. By then, hopefully, he would no longer be in Cuba.

After a deep breath, contact with Langley was accomplished; he sent his message quickly and shut down the transmitter.

Langley's overseas communications personnel decrypted the message, routed it internally, and forwarded it to NSA and Naval Security Group HQ (OP-20-G).

Salvador got up, stretched, and did 30 pushups to burn some energy and calm down. He wiped his brow, sat down, and began searching the UHF and VHF bands for voice circuits. Since those bands have essentially line-of-sight ranges, they could not be monitored from U.S. soil. The *USS OXFORD*, an intelligence-gathering auxiliary ship patrolling off the northwestern coast of Cuba, was out of range of communications on those frequencies coming from Havana or Santa Cruz. Havana was a doubtful target for Salvador since it was about 25 miles away. A strong base station was expected to be heard, but less powerful mobile sets would surely be impossible to hear. Santa Cruz was a different story since it was less than two miles distant as the crow flies.

Any intelligence he discovered by monitoring line-of-sight circuits would be unique, highly valued by Washington, and all risks considered, the reason he was here.

Sorting through audible signals was somewhat tedious. Salvador began compiling a list of active voice frequencies, whether Cuban or Soviet-controlled, and their apparent purpose. He created a catalog of pertinent details and a net diagram of the callsigns for each circuit of interest. A simple filing system was created, comprised of overlapping stacks of papers on the end of the radio table. The stacks were based on the callsign of the net control of a circuit so he could quickly refer back or update information.

That being accomplished, little time passed before he discovered a new circuit on the second pass through the UHF and VHF frequency bands. Despite being weak, it was understandable. He cataloged and diagrammed it. Notes were made as an agitated Soviet demanded unmercifully that a Soviet officer at the Havana docks expedite the unloading of Soviet troops and cargo from a ship that arrived late the previous day. When that circuit became inactive, he searched and cataloged other voice circuits, finding several he flagged for priority attention.

Interrupted only briefly for simple meals and the bathroom, the rest of the day was spent collecting information in his attic lair, a hot tin can. He logged the names and cargoes of several Soviet ships that delivered food, grain, troops, trucks, cranes, patrol boats, and military crates.

Late evening conversations from a Soviet control station in Havana were significant because the chatter revealed secret cargo in large crates being loaded onto specifically configured trucks.

Strong signals emanating from the Santa Cruz area yielded mainly routine Soviet Army technician chatter. There was one brief reference to a weapon transporter, which piqued his interest. He hoped, in vain, that somewhere in that conversation, a specific weapon would be mentioned. There was Human Intelligence that Soviet Luna and FKR-1 surface-to-surface, or anti-ship, mobile missile systems were crated and shipped to Cuba. Before he left Washington, neither system had been photographed on ships or on the ground. Any circuits involved in those systems were his top priority.

As the evening progressed, voice circuit activity decreased significantly. At midnight, Salvador encrypted a lengthy report of the first day's significant intercepts, transmitted the information to CIA Langley, and went to bed. He tossed and turned on top of the sheet in only his skivvy shorts. Falling asleep was difficult with the discomfort of a hot, stuffy room, combined with the consternation of transmitting again and the excitement of the day's intercept activities. The lingering exhaustion from the previous night's swim and trek to the garage, with little sleep afterward, finally had its way with his mind and body.

After sleeping more than eight hours, Salvador quickly devoured a now cold breakfast that awaited him just inside the door. After a quick trip downstairs to the bathroom, he went directly to the radio table and went to work. It had been a busy morning of searching and logging significant chatter of Cubans and Soviets when Tomas brought lunch at 12:30.

Finished with his meal, he put on overalls and listened quietly for a few moments from a slightly ajar attic door. Hearing only the sound of light rain on the corrugated steel roof, Tomas' wrenches, and other mechanical noises, he proceeded down the stairs.

"Hello," Tomas said, briefly lifting his head from a Chevy's engine innards. "Sleep well?"

"Hello, Tomas, I did, eventually. I was dead tired," Salvador replied with a wave of his hand and went quickly into the bathroom. A few minutes later, the sound of a car stopping outside the garage sent chills up Salvador's spine. He hoped never to encounter anyone, but he knew it would happen. Just not so soon. The car's engine stopped, and a car door slammed. A man speaking Spanish with a heavy Russian accent entered the open side of the bays and engaged Tomas.

"Good afternoon, I need a headlight, two if you have them," said the Soviet. "Come take a look."

"No need to look, sir. I have no headlights. If you bring them, I can install," said Tomas.

"Do you know where I can find them?" the man said gruffly with obvious frustration. "I bought this American car last week with only one headlight working, and that one burned out last night. After ten days in your country, I find that you have nothing, nothing. It's worse than I thought. We will have to bring everything we need."

"I'm sorry that you have come while my country is having a hard time. But we all hope that Russia will help us, sir," Tomas said with an award-winning act of sincerity. "I think the larger garages in Havana can help you."

The Soviet turned and left, mumbling as he avoided muddy puddles from a passing shower.

Once the sound of the car's engine faded, Salvador came out of the bathroom. "His formal Spanish was good, Tomas. That's worrisome. Was he a civilian?"

"No, he was wearing a Soviet Army officer's uniform, but I don't know their uniform insignia. And yes, he didn't just have a crash course in Spanish. That, being able to travel alone and with a pretty good car, makes me think he may be KGB. My Cuban accent seemed to give him a little trouble. His facial expressions showed he wasn't used to our dialect yet. But then, he said he's only been here 10 days. Let's hope he doesn't come back."

"If he came here, he must have struck out with garages in Santa Cruz."

Tomas nodded, "He must belong to a unit somewhere in this general area, probably that airport I mentioned. They don't put KGB or fluent Spanish speakers in small units."

"I can't help but wonder how in the hell he found your little garage," said Salvador, shaking his head.

"Mmhmm, that bothers me much, Sergio. He must have gotten information from a Cuban official in this area."

Director of the CIA, John McCone, and JFK's National Security Advisor, McGeorge "Mac" Bundy, entered the Oval Office together, toting leather folders.

"Good afternoon, Mr. President," McCone said.

"Remains to be seen," JFK said while flashing his brilliant smile.

20

"Walter Heller was just in here with an update on some economic issues, so I'm hoping you're bringing me something more cheery." He pointed toward the sitting area.

"Mr. President, for background," said Bundy as he sat on the couch, "earlier this morning, I called John and asked him if there was any explicit confirmation for any of the communications intelligence we've been getting. Specifically, that which suggests offensive systems coming into Cuba, which reconnaissance photography hasn't confirmed. Something to get past the terms of probable and possible that they use to qualify their analytical points. Nothing so far is concrete evidence. I thought you should hear his answer."

"OK. It's been a long busy week, and it's only Wednesday, John," said JFK, leaning back, rocking gently in his chair. "Jackie just called down, and I told her I'd be another half hour. But I'm anxious to hear what you have to say."

McCone sat forward, mindful of the time allotment he'd just been given, and began, "The photographic intelligence analysts don't use the term probable unless they have firm comparative measurements and physical pattern data to support it. So far, Soviet military construction sites in Cuba are physically consistent with Soviet military defensive missile systems. As you know, that's changed our airborne reconnaissance approach." He opened his folder and scanned bullet points on the top page of his notes. "All that being said, I must tell you that there are some tentative indications that both offensive and defensive missile systems are being shipped, perhaps some recently arrived. The Navy is particularly concerned about indications that Komar Class patrol boats have or will be shipped. They will probably be equipped with two Termit anti-ship conventional missiles. We also have photographs of early site preparation at several locations that appear to be for air defense missile systems, which I mentioned previously. The extent of their defensive systems is telling. All that does, however, remain to be seen."

JFK frowned and stopped rocking, "That's not good news, but it's not firm proof of anything. Focus on verifying the presence of truly offensive systems—nuclear weapons. Kruschev himself strongly insisted there's nothing offensive going in there."

"My gut says otherwise, Mr. President, as you know," said McCone.

"You're in the minority of our advisors," Bundy said with a grin.

"That may be so, but the circumstantial evidence is too strong. I'll just say that I can't imagine Kruschev not wanting a ground-based ballistic missile system with range of the U.S. and with an all too willing Castro, Cuba is easily obtained prime real estate."

"That would upset the nuclear deterrence posture, but I wouldn't put it past the Soviets to make such a bold move. We just need the irrefutable goods on Kruschev before we can confront him," said Bundy.

"Exactly," said JFK.

McCone nodded, "With U-2 reconnaissance aircraft and communications and electronic intelligence telling us where to look and for what, we'll get it. Speaking of communications intelligence. We believe the first truly offensive missile systems to be deployed will be the short-range tactical nuclear SSMs or surface-to-surface missile systems. They would be their protection against a naval invasion. In that regard, we recently developed an in-country source focused on that problem. That source has been reporting unique COMINT about Soviet ship offloading. They are also alert for any Soviet radio communications pertinent to SSM or other offensive missile systems."

Bundy interjected, "We're still talking communications intelligence, John. The WWII deception plans for Normandy were incredibly successful. They made phony communications networks and military bases look like something they were not. The damn Soviets could be doing the same thing to us. Perhaps to test us out, to see how we react. If we let it pass, they'll bring in the real thing. That, gentlemen, would strengthen their strategic and negotiating positions by orders of magnitude. You already told me that the Soviet merchant ships are filing falsified shipment and movement reports. They know we're listening to them."

"Yes, Mac, but we have U-2 high-altitude reconnaissance aircraft that can follow up on COMINT and give us good pictures," said McCone. "We also have highly trusted Cuban informants, in and near Havana and elsewhere, that get ground truth from resistance rings. Even that's not easy, though, because the Soviets kicked all the Cubans out of the ports and put a tight security perimeter around the military constructions sites."

JFK nodded, "You two keep your heads together on offensive

missiles in Cuba and keep me informed. I've told Defense and State that I don't want any hints of offensive systems in Cuba getting to the press. Reporters already know there's a Soviet buildup going on. They're suspicious of it, and rightly so. They'll be digging hard for more details. No leaks, gentlemen, no leaks!"

4 – Visitors

All appearances of a peaceful early morning in the garage were present. Still, Salvador lingered at the door for sounds other than Tomas before going down to use the bathroom.

Tomas was lying on a dolly under a car. He heard Salvador coming down the steps and called out, "Sergio, just the man I need."

"Hello, Tomas. What do you need?"

"I could use some help here when you can,"

"I'll be right out."

A few minutes later, Salvador left the bathroom and stood by Tomas' feet, sticking out from under the car. "OK, what can I help you with?"

"I have no other dolly, but please slide under from the other side of the car and hold this muffler in place while I attach hangers."

Salvador got down and pulled himself under the opposite side of the car. "How's this?" he asked, holding onto the muffler.

"Perfect, hold it right there."

"What happened, Sergio, was that the old hangers rusted out, and the muffler dropped to the road. They didn't drag it far. Luckily it was a dirt road. They tied it back up with rope and brought it in. I removed all the old hangers and am putting in new ones. Now we just need to put the muffler and pipes back in place."

Sergio laughed, brushing away rust or dirt that dropped onto his face, "I can see the muffler is dented and scraped. It's a miracle the pipes didn't separate."

"They did; I had to weld them back together." As Tomas attached hanger straps to the exhaust pipe leading to the muffler, a man entered the bay, calling out in a natural-born Cuban accent, "I came early to watch you finish my car."

Dark brown leather shoes and tan linen trousers were all Salvador could see when he looked over from under the car.

"I'll be done in about 20 minutes, Doctor Luis," said Tomas.

"I see your mechanic came back."

Tomas chuckled, "No, this is my new man, Sergio."

"Oh, very good! I am Doctor Luis Basilio, Sergio. What is your last name?"

"Lopez, I'm pleased to meet you, Doctor," he called out from under the car.

"Sergio Lopez, hmm," said Luis, pausing.

Salvador was unnerved as Luis began pacing slowly as he spoke.

"I haven't heard that name around here," Luis continued. "You must be new to this area, at least to the Camilo Cienfuegos area. Your accent sounds like one from the eastern end of Cuba. Where did you grow up?"

"On a farm near Los Reynaldos," said Salvador, repositioning under the car to get a different grip as Tomas installed tailpipe hangers.

"What larger city is that near?" asked Dr. Luis.

"Guantanamo, our farm was about 30 kilometers west of that."

"I just hired him this week," Tomas interjected to deflect Luis' questioning of Salvador. "He's working for shelter and food until he gets on his feet here."

Dr. Luis continued, "I see. Sergio, do you have relatives here?"

"No," Salvador said with a laugh. "That would sure make it easier for me."

"Are you married?" Luis asked with a serious, probing tone of voice.

"No, Doctor, I am not." Can't he see I'm under this car working? His curiosity is getting annoying; no, it's worrisome.

"Have you ever been?"

"No, sir," Salvador said with a grunt while repositioning.

"You like women, though?"

I'm beginning to dislike this guy a lot. "For sure, but the right woman has not come along, Doctor."

"I see. What can you do other than work on cars, Sergio?"

Salvador suppressed a smile, thinking, Oh, wouldn't he like to know? "I'm just a mechanic, cars, trucks, things with engines."

"There's a lot of that work around here," Luis said matter of factly. "How about tires? I'm sure you can patch flat tires. When I left the clinic to walk over here, they told me our ambulance had a flat. I'll give you a ride to the clinic when my car is done so you can fix it."

Tomas didn't like that idea, took a deep breath, and interrupted, "I'll grab the things to patch it and ride over with you, Doctor Luis," said Tomas. "I want Sergio to stay and get started on an electrical problem with that other car," said Tomas. "I learned that he's much better with a car's electrical things than I am."

That afternoon, Salvador heard Tomas' 2-2 knock on the attic door to deliver lunch. Salvador took off his headphones and called out, "Come in!"

"It's so hot up here!" Tomas said, putting a small tray on the table. "You can open the front and back windows during the day for cross ventilation. But do it from the side of the window somehow, not in front of it. If I didn't tell you that before, I apologize."

"Thank you. That will be a big help. If you have a few minutes, I'd like to ask you about Dr. Basilio," Salvador said as he sat at the table to get started on lunch of a cold chicken wing, two slices of bread, and a small cup of coffee. He motioned for Tomas to sit. "These wings from one of your chickens?"

"Yes, Sergio. When they stop laying eggs, we eat them. The eggs are more valuable to trade than eating them," he laughed. "I wanted to talk to you about Luis. He is the Director of the health clinic in town, which makes him an important government official by the nature of that position. He is a source of information about this area to the government. That's why I didn't want you to go to the clinic with him. It would give him time to question you for more details. He's intelligent and cunning, and he would eventually find a flaw or something suspicious in an answer."

With the last bits of meat gnawed from the bones, Salvador wiped his fingers on the hand towel that came with the tray. "I thought that's what was going on. It was more than a few social questions. When I crawled out from under the car and made eye contact with him, it sent a little chill through me. I didn't see friendly eyes."

"Your instincts are good, Sergio. I have to be really careful with him. Listen, I've been thinking. We better put a box of parts up here for you to carry down from this storage area as a ruse. If he comes back when you're up there and wonders where you are, I can yell up to ask if you've found the parts. That would be your cue to get your coveralls on and bring the box down. You can yell some answer that gives you time to get ready to come down. That would also be a good thing to do for anyone else that comes in like that."

"Good idea!"

"OK, I'll put a box of parts together after dinner and bring them up when I come back for your tray and laundry bag. Oh, I have a five-gallon can for you to use for burning papers. A patch of window screen material is inside it. Two boxes of matches are also in the can. It's at the bottom of the stairs. You can bring it up next time you go to the bathroom."

On Friday, August 17, 1962, CIA Director John McCone arrived at the West Wing of the White House bright and early to give JFK the Presidential Daily Brief of intelligence. National Security Advisor McGeorge "Mac" Bundy was already present in the Oval Office.

"Good morning, Mr. President...Mac," McCone greeted.

JFK motioned toward the couch, "Have a seat, John, and let's have it. I have a tight schedule. After this, I'm leaving for South Dakota. They want me to inspect the Oahe Dam Power Project."

"First off, Mr. President, we have intelligence that the Soviets are making rapid progress on what appear to be surface-to-air missile sites at several locations. The details are in the daily folder."

"Don't we have good coverage from the photo-reconnaissance satellites?" asked Bundy, continuing, "I haven't heard you mention that source so far. We've spent millions on the ground and space systems for those things."

JFK cocked his head slightly, focused on the response.

McCone cleared his throat, "The recon sats are more strategic than tactical. It often takes a couple weeks or so to get results from them. When the film canisters in the satellites are full, they are ejected into space with parachutes and recovered in mid-air by specially configured aircraft. That's a lot of film for the photo interpreters to analyze, so that takes time. I should add that the satellite images we've received to date haven't given us anything that adds to or contradicts our reports based on what we've seen from reconnaissance flights. Satellites are more strategic than a tactical resource."

JFK and Bundy both nodded understanding.

"Of interest, we have several communications intelligence sources referring to a quote, mobile launcher, unquote, which we strongly believe are for those anti-ship missile systems."

Bundy interrupted. "Believe…but no photography of any kind on mobile launchers yet, I take it?"

"No, regrettably, but analysts are scouring all the films we get for them and for anything else offensive, for that matter," said McCone.

JFK sat forward in the rocking chair, "I'll be stopping in several states during the next few days, but don't hesitate to call me by secure phone on Air Force One if you come up with anything more on offensive weapons. I'll return to the White House on the 20th. Get on my schedule late that afternoon for an update. Please continue."

"Yes, Mr. President. The next item on the PDB regards an interesting incident yesterday in Moscow, reported by the CIA Chief of Station…"

The sun was just above the horizon this quiet Saturday morning. Salvador's situps, pushups, breakfast, and a bathroom visit were already out of the way. He sat on the stool at the radio desk, crossed off Friday, August 17th, on his homemade calendar, and took a deep breath. It sure feels like I've been on this island for more than five days. I sure miss my life in Homestead. For a fleeting moment, he visualized Angela having breakfast and getting ready to go to work. He energized his receivers and put on his headphones. The frequencies for the top three priority voice circuits were quiet. He began monitoring the chatter on the frequency of the Soviet control station on the Havana dock cargo handling coordination circuit. The details for the morning offloading plan for the Soviet merchant ships Sevastopol, Severoles, and Kislovodsk contained military cargo that was unspecified but still worthy of reporting to Langley. When that circuit became quiet, he rechecked the frequencies of his top-priority circuits while searching for new ones.

Mid-morning, Salvador heard his top priority Santa Cruz circuit become active. Hoping to hear more about the 'launcher' mentioned previously, he focused intently on every word. Come on, guys, give me what I'm looking for. He took notes on the network's discussion of today's maintenance tasks for three mobile launchers. Whether they were for anti-ship or anti-aircraft missiles remained to be seen. The network became quiet before he got an answer to that question. Damn it, guys! Maybe the analysts can glean something from the jobs they talked about.

Later that morning, the sounds of a car pulling up to the garage diverted Salvador's focus. He pulled one earphone from his ear to hear what was happening below, splitting his attention with the Russian voices in the other ear. Tomas was busy working on a car in the bay, making familiar bangs and clanks. But the slam of a car door, then a voice in the bay below, created an adrenalin dump. That was an accent Salvador knew all too well, but a different voice than the man looking for headlights. He quietly removed his headphones, shut down his radios, grabbed the pistol, and stood by the cot, dead still, listening at full alert.

"Good morning, sir. I haven't met you yet," said Tomas.

"Major Melnikov," the man said. "I have an electrical problem. Rear lights." The deep gruff voice was unnerving, even in good Spanish. But coming from a senior Soviet officer made it alarming.

"We can work on that, Major. Can you leave the car? I can take you back to your base and come back later. It may be two hours before we can be done."

"No," the Soviet replied abruptly. "I will wait. Get started right away. I hear you have an expert electrician. I want him to work on it."

"As you wish, Major."

Tomas cupped his hands at his mouth and yelled toward the stairs, "Sergio, did you find those parts yet?"

"Yes! They were hard to find," Salvador yelled back. "I'll be right down." He put the weapon in the side table drawer, quickly slipped on overalls, put on work boots, picked up the box of parts, and went downstairs. Seeing the Soviet Army Officer's uniform sent a chill down his spine. Oh, shit. This is a nightmare.

"Is that the expert electrician?" asked the Major. "My brake lights aren't working. Come take a look."

The Major's mention of an expert electrician gave both Salvador and Tomas pause; Dr. Basilio and the Major must have been talking.

"Stop working on the other car, Sergio, and work on the Major's lights," Tomas said with authority.

"Sure, I'll see what I can find," said Salvador. I wish I had taken some acting classes. I've got to be really careful with this guy.

The Major got in the car and hollered, "I am pressing the brake pedal. The lights should come on, yes?"

Salvador watched at the rear of the car and called out, "You are correct; the brake lights are not coming on."

"Open the trunk, please, sir," said Salvador.

"Address me as Major!" he barked as he came to the rear of the car with a ring of keys and unlocked the trunk.

"Thank you, Major." Heaven forbid that I just call him sir. I'm hating this guy and all Soviets even more.

Salvador opened the trunk and discovered that the lid wouldn't stay up. Holding the lid up with one hand, he inspected the wires going to the taillights. "Oh, it looks like rough roads jolted the wire loose that goes to both lights," he said matter-of-factly. "I'll get something to prop this lid up so I can work." He could at least hold the damn lid, but no, that would be beneath the Major. Asshole! Calm down, Sal.

The Major curtly nodded but did not try to hold the lid up. Salvador closed the trunk and went to the garage. Tomas overheard the conversation and handed Salvador a broomstick and screwdriver.

F'n Major is watching every move I make. Salvador returned to the car, "OK, Major, this will work. It won't take me long. I only need to reconnect one wire, and you can be on your way. I'll be done in a few minutes."

"There can't be a payment for such a fast repair!" said the Major.

Tomas heard that and walked over. "Major, this is a proud socialist garage. There is never a charge."

The Major smiled. "I will return in a few days to make sure the lights have been fixed good." He got into the car, slammed the door shut, and drove away.

"That wire was purposely disconnected," said Salvador.

Tomas smiled, "I don't doubt that. He knew you'd find the problem right off, so his purpose today was just to see if you actually had electrical skills after somehow getting a rundown from our friend Dr. Luis. He probably has his staff trying to find out if the local police know something about you."

"Being suspect is not good. I'm not anxious to have him come back."

"Yes! I don't like how this is going either." Tomas pointed at the box of parts Salvador brought down, still sitting on a workbench, "He didn't see what was in there, so take it back upstairs."

Salvador returned to the loft, already uncomfortably hot from the sun beating down unmercifully on the steel roof. He got out of the overalls and boots. He toweled his sweaty face, arms, and chest and returned to the radio table. Resuming the monitoring routine, the top priority UHF band circuit was active. Soviet Army technicians at different locations were talking about who was being sent to the docks in Havana tomorrow to pick up Luna equipment. That made his heart skip a beat as he scribbled the conversation verbatim onto the intercept log sheet. Later in the afternoon, Soviet troops were chatting excitedly about being selected to take three FKRs from Havana to Guantanamo and help finish setting up the base there. Hearing 'FKR' sent enough adrenalin through him that his fingers quivered slightly as he copied the exact words of this chatter onto the intercept log. Bingo! I got your asses. Hearing the nomenclature for a Soviet surface-to-surface missile put a smile on his face. He knew that tonight's report would set off a lot of fires in DC. Monitoring any other frequency for the rest of the weekend was out of the question—more details would surely be revealed by the chatty Soviets.

31

5 – Smoke and Fire

Two days later, Marvin Jefferson began Monday morning early at CIA HQ, Langley, VA. He sat down at his cluttered desk to enjoy a mug of black coffee while reading documents in the folder marked 'urgent' that his secretary had brought to him. The top sheets in the file were Salvador's reports transmitted Saturday and Sunday night. Three items in those reports got his attention. One was the intercept of chatter between two Soviet soldiers and a Soviet officer, which mentioned a team of men assigned to pick up two Luna launchers in Havana harbor. Another was chatter on that circuit that referred to taking Luna systems to Guantanamo. The third, also from that circuit, was a reference to officers and soldiers arriving in three days with some FKR systems.

Jefferson reached for his secure phone. He dialed..."Good morning, boss! I'm sending up copies of COMINT reports you need to see right away. They're from Cymbal Beat. There's great stuff in them. There are Luna mobile anti-ship missiles in Cuba now and others with longer range, FKR-1s, all arriving in a couple days. Our gamble with that op has paid off...Alright, boss, I'll get started on the briefing boards and narrative right away...oh, I don't know, that depends on the graphics arts weenies, but I'd say later this afternoon, OK?...got it, boss. I'll call as soon as it's all ready."

Jameson Donnelly, Chief of the Cuban Analysis Group at the National Security Agency, Fort George G. Meade, MD, no sooner sat down at his desk when his secure phone rang. "Donnelly...Good morning Marvin... Yes, it was a good weekend. We went to Ocean City. How was yours?... Not yet. I just walked in...what? Lunas and FKRs?...Yes, it sure is...I'll find those reports and call you back...Oh, OK, I can see the value in moving him, and I suppose it would be less risky now than it would be later on when the island will be crawling with Ruskies. But we'd lose what we're getting from Santa Cruz... I'm sure Gitmo could give us something useful... Why don't we see what the Naval Security Group thinks..."

McGeorge "Mac" Bundy, JFK's National Security Advisor, returned to his office from lunch in the West Wing dining room. He ran his hand back over his receding hairline and dove into his never empty in-basket. His concentration was interrupted by the intercom when his secretary announced that John McCone, Director of the CIA, was on the secure phone.

"This is Mac, good afternoon John...That's significant, alright...Any reconnaissance photos of them?...Here we go again with COMINT. I hesitate to brief the President on this information alone. As I've said before, they could be baiting us with a clever deception...When do you think you'll have some pictures?...OK, I'll take that under advisement...Thanks, John."

Salvador recognized the sound of Major Melnikov's car pulling up in front of the garage. That engine had a unique sound along with a stuttered shutdown which he figured was probably due to an ignition timing problem or delayed fuel shut-off relay. He turned off the radios, got into his coveralls, looked through the box of parts they staged, and grabbed one that was plausible for the job he knew Tomas was working on. He put on the overalls and waited cautiously by his cot, pistol in hand, listening.

"Stop looking for that part and come down," Tomas called out. "The

Major is back for you to check his car."

"I found one, Tomas. Coming down."

"Good! I was sure I had one up there," Tomas replied loudly.

The Major was pacing as Salvador came down the stairs.

The Major looked up at Salvador, "There is the man I want to talk to."

"Major, I can check the brake light wires for you. He's got an important electrical problem to find on this other car," said Tomas.

"No, no," the Major said gruffly, shaking his head with disgust. "Return to your work. I want Sergio to recheck my wires."

"Don't keep him from his work long, Major," said Tomas as he accepted the part from Salvador, hiding concern about the Major's real reason for his interest in Salvador.

Major Melnikov gestured to Sergio, "Come make sure those wires are still connected properly."

Salvador followed the Major to the rear of the car. This is bullshit. Typical Soviet blatant bullshit. He's up to something. He gives me the creeps. It's like playing with matches near gasoline.

As he unlocked the trunk, the Major asked, "Have you always lived in Cuba?"

Salvador lifted the trunk lid and checked the wiring. I better fill in some blanks with my cover story to turn this curiosity off. "No, I went to Miami as a teenager. I didn't stay long. I signed onto a merchant ship that was based in Barcelona. When it docked in Havana several years later, I quit and stayed." He closed the trunk lid. "The wiring looks perfect, Major. They won't rattle loose again."

"Where did you learn your mechanical and electrical skills?"

Salvador fought off the urge to shiver at the Major's cold expression and penetrating dark brown eyes that seemed to be painfully piercing his brain. "I worked on cars as a young kid, but a lot of it came from working in the Engineering Departments aboard ship."

Without a word, Major Melnikov turned with a nod, got in his car, and drove off.

"That was not fun," said Salvador as he walked to the stairs.

"Not good, Sergio. This is not good."

A busy day for everyone had come to an end. Tomas' wife cleared the dinner table and began washing the dishes while he settled into the old battered wicker chair he inherited from his parents. Barely past the front page, someone knocked at the front door.

Tomas knew from the knock pattern that it was his anti-Castro cell boss, Marco Castaneda, also a CIA contact.

"Good evening, Tomas! I just came for a short talk," said Marco.

"Come in, Marco." Tomas motioned toward the dinner table.

"Good evening, Dalita," Marco called out, hearing her in the kitchen.

"Good evening, Marco. Can I get you something?" asked Dalita.

"No, thank you. I won't be here long."

Tomas and Marco waited for Dalita to go into the bedroom. She went there when Marco visited, so she could not hear their conversation. She knew that the less she knew, the better.

"I think we have a problem with your visitor, Tomas," said Marco.

Tomas nodded, but before he could comment, Marco continued, "My contact in Dr. Basilio's clinic said a Soviet officer visited the doctor in his office this afternoon. Most of the conversation was not very loud, but the words Sergio, Lopez, and Barcelona were mentioned. Also, something about a Spanish merchant ship in Havana."

"We do have a problem, Marco," Tomas said, shaking his head. "Dr. Basilio brought his car in for muffler repairs recently, which turned into a questioning of Sergio. Then Major Melnikov showed up with a tail light problem that was purposely created for Sergio to work on. That was the Major's chance to question Sergio while he worked. All those words you mentioned relate to Sergio's background cover story that came out during that conversation."

"We have no choice. He cannot be in your shop any longer. He's a danger to us. Come up with a story to cover his absence. I will return later tonight to pick him up and move him to a safe place. I'll return about, oh, 2 in the morning."

"Good! That will give him time to destroy his papers. What about the radio equipment?"

Marco paused, "Get it all down in the garage to be picked up tonight. Someone will come in a truck with me tonight to take it all out of here and dispose of it. Make sure you include any antenna wires. Your attic has to appear to be completely innocent. Just storage and his temporary living space."

Nodding, Tomas said, "Yes, of course."

"Do you think Sergio will give you any trouble about this?"

"No, he's very security conscious and has been unnerved by the questioning. He will understand."

"That's good. I will see you at 2."

Once Marco had departed, Tomas went into the garage, went up the stairs, and made his 2-2 knock on Salvador's door.

Salvador looked at his watch. 2010, what's he want this time of night. This can't be good. He took off his headset, picked up the pistol, and went to the door. "Hello, Tomas."

"Hello, Sergio. It's safe. Can I come in? We need to talk right away."

"Yes, sure!" said Salvador opening the door. "Come into my office."

Tomas didn't laugh or smile. They sat at the table in the dim light from the small lamp at the radio table. "Sergio, we're taking emergency action. We are all in danger. We have to move you to safety tonight at 2 a.m."

A rush of adrenalin invaded Salvador's gut, turning his face red and kicking up his heart rate. "I'll have to send a message right away." Move me to safety, he says. Sounds like I'm in real deep shit. "What happened? Where am I going?"

"The Major and the Dr. are too suspicious of you. It sounds like they're going to try to validate your cover story. I don't know where you're going, but you'll be safe there."

"Then what?"

"Sergio, I don't know. But you need to trust our people."

"Will this radio gear still be here for me to come back to or for the next guy?"

"You or nobody else will be up here. It is too dangerous now. So, my friend, you and I have to disassemble your radios and get your antennas out of the ceiling and rolled up. We're going to clean this place up and remove any evidence of activity. All your radios and other gear are going to be picked up tonight."

Damn, the shit is really hitting the fan, and I have no options for this. The operation plan is out the window now. I sure hope good old Marvin Jefferson can cook up a way to get my ass out of Cuba. He looked at his watch and looked up at Tomas, trying to find words.

"Sorry for the surprise, Sergio. Get into your civilian clothes. We need to get everything done by 2."

"Can I keep my pistol and ammo, just in case?"

"No! That's going with the radios, too. If you got caught with it, they would kill you. If you get stopped without it, you will at least have a chance of talking your way out of trouble."

Nodding reluctantly, Salvador said, "The first thing I need to do is transmit a message, then burn all my papers before working on the radios."

Salvador successfully contacted CIA Langley, transmitted an encrypted message describing his situation, and turned off power to all the radio gear. Tomas helped him loosely rumple pages of once precious material and toss them into the can, where they instantly caught fire from those already burning. It took only twenty minutes to turn the incriminating pages into ashes.

"Flush these ashes down the toilet," said Tomas. "You start dismantling your gear and put them by the doorway. I'll carry start carrying the items down into the garage."

6 – Down on the Farm

Tomas opened the side entrance door to the garage bays when he heard Marco's knock pattern. Marco entered and shut the door. Tomas turned on his red-lens flashlight.

Salvador noted that it was 1:50 a.m. Here we go, all downhill from here. God only knows what's in store for me. I love you, Angela.

Tomas put his hand on Salvador's shoulder and whispered, "This is Sergio."

The man offered Salvador a handshake and said softly, "I am Marco!"

"Did you get everything done?" Marco asked Tomas.

"Yes, boss, we have all the equipment and things in the bay, ready to go."

Marco looked directly into Salvador's eyes, showing no expression, "You will be taken to a safe place tonight. It's going to be a long walk. I hope you know how important this is." He pointed at the laundry bag Salvador had slung over his shoulder, "You must leave that behind. Your watch, too."

"It's just clean underwear."

Marco pointed at the floor, "The bag stays, Sergio."

Salvador nodded and dropped the bag, and handed Tomas his watch. "I'm ready," he said, feeling his heart racing and his skin burning.

Marco nodded, "I will take you part of the way. We'll meet a man who will take you the rest of the way. Let's go. Goodbye, Tomas. The truck will be here any minute for the things to be taken away."

Tomas turned off his flashlight and opened the door; Marco and Salvador departed quietly.

Salvador followed Marco silently along one isolated dirt road after another in eerie near-total darkness. An hour passed without seeing anyone. While walking, he allowed his mind to recall moments with Angela. I'm a lucky man to have her in my life. Oh, how I miss her. If I'm really lucky, I'll get to see her again. Dear God, see me through this. His mental imagery was broken when a curious dog came out of the darkness to greet them.

"Don't pay attention to it," whispered Marco.

The dog went from one to the other, jumping up to nip at their fingers and tugging their pants legs for several minutes, trying valiantly to get their attention. The dog gave up with a soft yip and left them.

Not long after that, Marco slowed down and whispered over his shoulder, "Someone is coming, but I'm expecting him about now. Be alert."

"Wonderful night for a moonlight walk," whispered the man, now 15 feet away.

"Yes, and the birds are singing," Marco whispered back.

Salvador relaxed, hearing an exchange of security code phrases.

Marco shook the man's hand, saying, "This is Sergio." He turned to Salvador and whispered, "Good luck to you."

As Marco left them, the man whispered, "I am Raúl. Come with me, Sergio." They shook hands vigorously. "We have an hour to walk. Let's hurry."

So began the rest of Salvador's brisk walk further east to a new hiding place. It was a meandering route of dirt roads past open farmland, undeveloped areas, and small settlements of houses and buildings, which were tucked in for the night without any lights showing. The silence was deafening. No birds or animals were about. Breathing and footsteps seemed loud against a muffled world.

Images and moments with Angela flowed through his mind as Salvador trudged quickly behind Raúl. They were sweet diversions that revitalized him. He smiled widely, enjoying the mental slide show. When his mind cleared of musings, he looked for his watch in force of habit. Damn, I wish I didn't have to give it up. He chuckled to himself, knowing that no Cuban or Soviet was likely to have one like it. Yeah, it would have been a dead giveaway. I wonder what Tomas did with it. Sure hope he didn't bury that too. I'd like to come back and get it as a souvenir. Seems like we've been walking for hours.

Raúl turned onto a path and whispered, "My house." Salvador could faintly see a house at the end of the rutted narrow dirt path. Aside from the sounds of their boots in the dirt, an intermittent breeze rustled young sugar cane leaves on stalks growing on each side of the path. The dull light in a front window was a subtle beacon that promised rest and safety, at least for now.

"Come in," whispered Raúl, pushing the front door open.

A small ceiling light illuminated a modest open room that served as a kitchen, dining room, and living room. In the center of the bare wood floor sat a four-place table with a folded newspaper and an overflowing ashtray. There was a back door to the yard. Another door, half-open, was for a small bedroom, which had just enough room for a bed and a chest of drawers. Screened windows on two sides of the main room were wide open, allowing a bug-free hint of cross-breeze to waft through intermittently.

He smokes cigars and cigarettes, Salvador thought as he sorted the stronger smells of them from the mustiness of a house open to hot, humid days. Now in light, he saw Raúl, a short, dark-skinned lanky man, standing patiently, watching Salvador regard the room.

Raúl was running his fingers through a full head of brown hair when he broke the silence, "I'm living alone right now because Laline, my wife, is in Jibacoa del Norte helping care for her aunt, who is very ill."

"I'm sorry to hear about that. How long will Laline be gone?"

Raúl's eyes teared, "Until they can get a hospital bed for her aunt if she lasts that long."

"Oh, how sad. I can see that means a lot to you. I'll say a prayer for your families every night."

"Thank you. That's very kind." Raúl paused for a moment to shake away sadness. "Back to our business. I have been told you are not permitted to leave this farm until you are moved again."

"Yes, I understand."

"What kind of work can you do?"

"I have worked on cars, car engines, and their electrical system, but I have never done any farm work."

"What farm work you can do for me, I can teach you. It would be good to have you help with that and the animals. There's so much work here."

"I'll help you, gladly."

"Good. You are lucky we're not harvesting. A machete would put blisters on those hands," Raúl said, pointing and chuckling.

Salvador laughed, "There is no doubt about that, sir!"

"I am sorry, but there is only one bedroom in this house. There's a little building out back that workers use during the sugar cane harvest. You can sleep there. There is an outhouse out there too. It's too late to get you settled in the worker's building, so you can sleep in one of those chairs," he pointed at two wicker rocking chairs with faded and cracking cowhide-covered cushions."

Salvador smiled, scratching his chin that itched from so many days without shaving. "It won't take me long to fall asleep, even if I have to lay on a bare floor. When do you harvest?"

"We will probably start in November. It will take about two months. I don't have big fields."

"Oh, I should be gone by then. What happens with me next, and when?"

"I don't know. Let's get some sleep. We'll talk more in the morning and get you settled in the other house."

Marvin Jefferson woke to the loud ringer of the bedside work phone at his apartment in McLean, Virginia. He glanced bleary-eyed at the alarm clock next to the bed; it said 3:19. "Jefferson!... Yeah, I'm awake now. Go ahead… Oh shit! OK, I'll be there in about 40 minutes."

It was 4:18 a.m. when Jefferson greeted the CIA Special Operations Control Center Duty Officer. "Mornin', Shirley, watcha got?"

"Good morning, Mr. Jefferson. Source Sergio sent a message out of normal schedule that reported his hideout was being sanitized, that his documents would be burned, and all radio equipment would be removed and disposed of. He is relocating to an unknown location at 0200. Nothing heard from anyone else about it. That's all we have right now, sir."

"Things were starting to get dicey there, but it sounds like it went sour. Alright. When did Sergio send his message?"

Shirley located the original message in a folder, "2048 last night."

"Why did you wait so long to call me?"

"Comm center said there was a garble in the encryption page settings, and it took them a long time to figure it out. I called you the minute I got it, sir."

"Alright. Did the message get sent to the Navy?"

She referred to the addressee list on the message form, "Yes, sir."

"Alright, Shirley, thank you. Update the status board to show that I'll be in my office twenty-four-seven until I advise otherwise."

Jefferson was still on his first CIA-logoed mug of coffee when the secure phone rang. "Jefferson!"

"This is Dan Patterson. Good morning, Marv."

"Mornin' Captain Dan. They got you up, too, huh?"

"Affirmative! I see there's a big problem with our guy in Cuba. I think we need to initiate the option of getting him to Gitmo ASAP."

"I was sitting here thinking about just that. That option has gotten complicated by the advent of such a rapid and large influx of Soviets. They're not just concentrating into the Havana area, as we expected. They're spreading out, distributing their assets, so to speak. Building sites all over the damn island."

"I noticed. The at-sea recovery option by sub is a bad bet now, Marv. He ditched his diving gear, so he probably couldn't avoid patrol craft during the time it would take him to swim three miles to meet a sub. They would most likely be discovered if he was taken by any boat that far out after dark. Trying that by day is out of the question."

"I agree, Dan. Our only possibility with any survivability chance is by car or bike to Gitmo. But I just looked at the map. He's about 500 miles from Gitmo with a straight string. That would be 600 or more on roads. The first and last parts of the route will be the riskiest for Soviet and

Cuban Army encounters. But, even in between, there are plenty of Castro's Army and civilian sympathizers that might get curious about a traveling stranger."

"As for a car, there's the fuel problem. Let's see, Marv, 600 miles and averaging maybe 15 miles per gallon, that's 40 gallons. Most of the cars there probably have a 10-gallon fuel tank. So that's probably four tanks of fuel, right, and could be seven or eight stops for fuel, food, rest."

Jefferson paused, "Good grief, it could be more stops than that because of rationing, and food will be next to impossible."

"Correct. There's no guarantee that they'd be successful in getting fuel at any particular stop. I'm starting to wish we never loaned him to you guys," Dan said with an uncomfortable chuckle.

"I'm sorry it's going south for your man. I was just thinking about how tough it would be to ride a bike that far in those circumstances. Nothing seems feasible or even survivable. The more I think about this, the more I think he might just have to stay put where they take him. At least until he or we can figure something out. I think he will stay alive and out of prison a hell of a lot longer doing that than with any other option we have right now."

"Damn! When will you find out where they're taking him?"

"I should hear from our contact soon. That channel is slow. I'll let you know when I do."

"OK, Marv. But let's not stop thinking of some way to get him out of there, preferably to Gitmo, sooner rather than later."

"Roger that. My boss is returning from overseas later this morning. I'll huddle with him as soon as I can about this development and see what he thinks."

43

7 – Here We Go

Two days later, the morning sun had risen high enough to shine its rays through an open window and put a disturbingly warm kiss on Salvador's face. It was nature's alarm clock. He rolled instinctively, not yet awake, to escape the glaring beam heating an eyelid. Sensing nearness to the outer edge of the wooden bunk, he jolted into consciousness. After stretching, yawning, and adjusting his skivvies, he put on shoes and used the outhouse. I wonder if today brings me some good news. It's, uh, Thursday, August 23. I need to make a calendar before I lose track. Angela crept into his mind. He smiled as he took the luxury of imagining her getting their breakfast together.

The crude worker's bunkroom consisted of an 18' x 14' room with a door on the front and a single window on each wall. Also on the back wall was a sink with a hand pump and a minimum-size stove. Each side wall had two rustic wooden bunks, thin mattresses, and small pillows. A sheet and pillowcase did little to hide odors from the many men who previously used the mattress and pillow. An unfinished wooden table was in the middle of the room, slightly unstable from a few loose joints. Four wooden straight-back chairs, all different from one another, sat sloppily on each side. He shook his head. This is hands down the worst quarters I've ever had.

"Good morning," said Salvador as he came through the door of Raúl's house.

"Good morning, Sergio. Breakfast is waiting for you on the table. Get yourself a glass of water. I ran out of coffee. I'll go to the market early on Saturday and get more."

"I'm sure it's rationed. How much can you get?"

"Yes, I get three ounces of coffee each per week for Laline and me. It doesn't last long, even though we make it last."

"I hope you're successful. My body craves coffee," Salvador said with a laugh. The well water tasted strongly of iron, which tinted the glasses, white plates, cups, and saucers a pale yellowish-brown shade. But it somehow tasted good. The intense thirst created by perspiring in the heat made it more palatable.

"I don't know what you are used to, Sergio, but when you want to take a bath, there's a tin tub and bucket on the back porch. I take the tub over by the firepit every Sunday afternoon, then fill it with well water that I heat in the bucket using a wood fire."

Salvador laughed, "I'm not used to that, but I will be. I'll take one every Sunday afternoon while the fire is still going."

Swallowing the last of a wolfed-down breakfast, such as it was, Sergio said, "I have gotten used to conserving water, but not cold showers." They both laughed.

"Sergio, I want you to know that I appreciate that you are helping me with the farm."

"Certainly! I'm not afraid of hard work. "

"I never seem to catch up, even when Laline is home. We can't afford to have children, so it's just been the two of us until they send me help to harvest. I sure need your help with my wife gone. Thank you."

"It's the least I can do for giving me a safe place to hide."

"Laline and I are not gun-fighting revolutionaries. But we hate what Fidel has done to our country. I used to make a good living selling my sugar cane, but now they just take it. My farm belongs to the people now. They just let me continue to live here and grow more cane for them."

"Which means you earn no pesos."

45

"Yes, no pesos! The manager of the central azucarero, the cane processing plant, gives me food, machetes, and supplies for the people that come here to harvest. But no money."

"How do you make a living then?"

"They just let me keep the small amount of meat and vegetables I grow. That's it. The farmers trade some things amongst themselves, but not often. We all have little. Basic things are free, so I don't need pesos. But what is available is rationed. The only people getting pesos are the military and authorities."

"That makes a hard life for you both, Raúl."

"That is why we do what we can for the cause when it's possible. When I was asked to bring you here, I didn't hesitate. I don't know where you came from or what you did, but I don't want to know. You talk like a Cuban, but not from around here."

Sergio smiled, "You're right about being better off. But I can't thank you enough for helping me. Hopefully, I won't be here very long. Do you see Cuban soldiers, police, or any Soviets in this area?"

"I have only seen the Cuban work soldiers and men that come in trucks when the sugar cane is ready to harvest. They haul it off to the plant that makes the sugar."

Marvin Jefferson's secure phone rang. He answered, "Jefferson."

"Good morning Marv! Dan Patterson. Admiral Kurtz and I just got back from NSA. Donnelly briefed us on the latest ground situation as they see it. After we got back to headquarters, the Admiral said, "I think we should get Conte to Gitmo before his situation becomes impossible."

"We talked about that before, Dan."

"I know. I know. I related the high points of our discussion to the Admiral. He listened, but what we heard at NSA was compelling. If we wait, he won't have any chance of getting out of there. The Cuban government isn't going to be defeated anytime soon. Not to mention that the island will be crawling with Ruskies real soon."

"I'll have to talk to my boss. The memo of understanding for this op gives us the final word, you know."

"The Admiral understands that and wants your boss to call him."

"Roger that, Dan. I'll be in touch."

It was 1:30 when Dan's secure phone rang. "Captain Patterson!"

"Good afternoon, Dan. Have a good lunch?"

"Yes, Marv, there was a farewell luncheon for one of my officers. I'm full as a tick. The Admiral just called me with an update. He told me he had his conversation with your boss, and a decision would be made shortly. You have news?"

"Yes, my boss bumped it up the chain to the Deputy for Ops. The short version of this story is that I've been directed to pull out all the stops and get your man to Gitmo."

"Oh, here we go. Do you need anything from me before I get started with this on my end?"

8 – The Map

Sergio was woken by droplets of water hitting his face. Rain was blowing gently against the screen above his bunk. He rose quickly and closed all the windows in the bunkhouse. After a dash to the outhouse, he washed his hands in the sink, wiped his face with his hands, and dried them on his skivvies. He went to the table where his makeshift calendar awaited attention. As a stubby pencil marked an X through Saturday, August 25, he thought, It's only been a short time, but it sure has dragged. How much longer will it be? I may as well make a sheet for September tonight. God only knows how many more it's gonna be. OK, Sal, go get breakfast and get this day started.

"Good morning, Sergio."

"A rainy Sunday morning to you, Raúl."

"Rain is good for the vegetable crops and grass for the cows. I never complain about it."

"I shouldn't either. Good thing it woke me up. Without the morning sun, there's no telling how long I would have slept. You wore me out yesterday."

"I won't today. On Sunday, all I do is feed and water the animals and rest. We could play cards later if you would like that. But two of them are missing."

Salvador laughed, "I'm glad you told me! Maybe I'll just go to bed early. Oh, I smell coffee."

"Yes, it's still hot. Help yourself. That's your breakfast on the table. I have already had mine. Then we'll go to the barn and get those chores out of the way."

Sergio sat down to breakfast with a short, small cup of strong, sweetened coffee and hungrily finished the last three inches of a bread loaf with a little rice and beans. "I suppose you haven't heard any news about me?"

"Sorry, Sergio, no news."

"Do you have regular contact with someone who will know?"

"Not regular, no. If they have something for me to know or do, they come here. I haven't seen anyone since they asked me to go get you."

"That was a risky thing for you to do."

"As I said before, I do things that will help get our country out of Castro's hands. It was a good thing that Laline wasn't here when they asked me to bring you here. She would have tried to make me refuse. She is so afraid that we'll be arrested for some of the things I have already done."

"You are a brave man, Raúl. I'm finished. I'll wash the cup, bowl, and spoon. Then let's go hit the barn."

After completing their work in the barn, Salvador and Raúl brought wood to the firepit and prepared for their evening baths.

Salvador towel-dried and then wrapped the towel around his waist. "You were right. That water gets cold fast."

Raúl laughed, "Makes you get the job done fast. This is the time when Laline and I take a little siesta, Sergio. You should do the same."

"That's a great idea, Raúl. I am very tired. If I sleep too long, just wake me. What's that? Do you hear it? A car is coming!"

Raúl pointed at the bedroom. "Go in the bedroom and close the door."

Sergio listened at the bedroom door, his mind racing through what he might do in different scenarios. I would feel a hell of a lot better if I had that pistol.

A knock at the door sent a chill down Sergio's spine. Then voices.

"Good morning, Humberto," Raúl said.

"Good morning. Is he here?" Humberto asked.

"Come out, Sergio."

Towel still wrapped around his waist, Salvador came out of the bedroom, ready to fight. He walked toward the table cautiously where Raúl and the visitor were standing. Is this a trap? Did Raúl rat me out?

"Hello, Sergio. I am Humberto. I have orders to get you to a new location early tomorrow morning." He turned to Raúl, "You should not hear the rest of this."

Nodding, Raúl said, "I'll be on the back porch."

More unsure of what was happening now, Salvador was ready for hand combat. I don't see any weapons. I can take him easy.

"Sergio, let's sit," said Humberto. Noting Salvador's hesitance to move, he sat down, clasped his hands on the table, and nodded.

Maybe this is on the up and up after all. My gut says go with it.

When Salvador sat down, Humberto said, "Listen carefully, Sergio. You're in safe hands. I will bring you a car at early light tomorrow for you to drive to the Navy base at Guantanamo. I have a camera in the car to get your picture and an ink pad to get your fingerprint. I need those to get a driver's license made for you. Are you willing to do that?"

He must be kidding. "You can do that by tomorrow morning? How about documents for the car? I can't get caught without those."

"Yes, I know that. We'll be working on that also this afternoon and evening. But we can do it. You will have what you need in case you are stopped. Nobody who stops you will know your identification and registration are not valid."

"I won't leave without those papers, Humberto."

"Do not worry. We have done this before."

Salvador nodded, still doubtful that it wasn't a car to drive that was coming tomorrow morning. I sure hope he's really going to help me get out of Cuba and is working with people that won't turn me in.

Humberto went to the car to get the equipment to take photographs and get thumbprints.

Salvador's mind remained alert, ready to act in case it was a weapon Humberto brought from the car. It was reassuring when a camera and a small wooden case came back with Humberto.

"These prints all look good. Let's go through the plan for the trip in great detail."

"You did say that I'm driving by myself, correct?"

"Yes, Sergio, it's best for you to travel alone and only during daylight. That will be much less suspicious."

"How about a suitcase and the normal things to travel with?"

"I was getting to that. I will bring a suitcase and some travel items on Monday. You already have the clothes you wore to get here. Raúl can give you some other things for you to put in the suitcase too."

"Good. How many miles will it be to the Naval Air Station? I think that will be the closest and safest for me," Salvador said, recalling his option planning at CIA HQ.

"I agree with you. That is your safest destination and route. It will be about 600 miles. I see the worry on your face, Sergio. You'll have about 13 hours of daylight. So, you can make it in two days if everything goes as planned."

Damn, this is not going to be a picnic. "That will take a lot of luck, but I have to take my chances."

Humberto nodded, reached inside his shirt, pulled out a map, and spread it out on the table. "You should be able to make it all the way to this location before dark Monday night. It is a safe place to stop for the night." Humberto's finger was on a city labeled Victoria de las Tunas. "There is a gas station there that is operated by a friend of our cause. It's more than halfway, but I think it is best for you to try to make it there tomorrow, even if it is close to dark by then. That will make it easier for you to get to Guantanamo the next afternoon."

Salvador examined the map quickly. "Are there any roads to avoid?"

"Yes! That's what you must understand completely. Follow my finger and memorize this route." He put his index finger on the map, "This is where you are now."

"Oh, I wondered about that. I can remember what you will show me, Humberto. Go ahead."

"I will show you the safest route. There will be enough gasoline stops," Humberto said as his finger slowly slid along an indirect route to the evening stopping point. "It's important that every time you get down near three-quarters of a tank, stop at the next gas station you see. Most will give you at least one gallon. But don't argue or try to convince them to give you more. You might have a station refuse to give you even a drop. Remember, these stations are government-controlled. They don't know you and won't do anything to jeopardize themselves. Just follow the three-quarter tank rule and keep stopping to be sure not to run out."

"I understand."

"You can see that some areas have few route choices due to the terrain and other things. That will make those areas more at risk for being stopped because of more traffic by government vehicles."

Salvador followed Humberto's finger as it moved slowly along the remainder of the route and stopped well short of the Naval Air Station.

"That is northwest of the Air Station, a few miles maybe," said Salvador. "What then?"

"That's the last thing I need to tell you about." Humberto reached into his shirt again for a hand-drawn high-detail map of an access point to the Navy property. "Stop back here, in this wooded area. Abandon the car, and walk along the road toward the gate. The Cuban Army constantly patrols the road that runs along the fence line. Hide at the edge of the woods so you can time the patrol pattern. Move up the road to the gate between those Army patrols. There's a U.S. Marine guard tower here by the gate. Here's the difficult part. These dots by the gate are the last known locations of land mines. These mines here are Cuban. Those along the fence are U.S. mines."

Salvador's heart began racing. "That's a lot of mines. Oh my God. How likely are those locations still good?"

"The source of them says they don't change."

"I'll cross my fingers. All the good that will do."

"Please notice the pattern of the mine locations. That you must remember. You can walk a safe path through them to get close enough to get the attention of the Marines. Stop as soon as they see you and follow their directions. That's when you'll need to convince them of who you are and to let you in before the next patrol comes by."

"I have to ask, sir, if you know. Where did the location of these dots come from?"

Humberto shrugged his shoulders, "I drew this myself from a Cuban government document. Just focus on the road to the gate and remember that pattern."

A shiver went through Salvador's core. "Let me study this for a minute."

"Of course. This is a lot to remember," Humberto said and sat back.

"I think I have it. What other surprises do you have?"

"I'll go through this twice, or as many times as you need, Sergio. Just do not mark this map. You must make this trip from memory. If you get stopped, you don't want to reveal your route, especially your destination."

"I understand," Salvador whispered with his gut churning.

"Good." Humberto reached into his pocket and pulled out an old leather watch. The old and dry leather strap had many cracks from age, and the crystal face was scratched. "This will help you keep track of the time. It's an old cheap one that is common here in Cuba."

"Thank you! I have missed having a watch."

"I'll show you the route again. Watch closely."

Sergio focused intently on Humberto's finger and detailed comments as he retraced the route.

"I won't breathe easy until I go through that Navy gate."

"Do you need me to show you again?"

"No, I have it. It's mostly intuitive, aside from a few places, but I have a good memory.

"Sergio, you must be alert and ready for anything to happen at any time. Being unarmed, you will only have quick thinking to keep you out of trouble."

"Oh, believe me, I know I'll get stopped and questioned at least once. The chance of not having problems of any kind is small, tiny, close to zero." Heat rushed to Salvador's cheeks at the specter of the many things that could go wrong.

Humberto's face became sullen. "We think the last 50 miles will be the riskiest part of the trip. There are many military, militia, and police forces in that area. Just don't panic if you get stopped and questioned.

"I'll be thinking all the while I'm driving about what to say about any question I can dream up."

"If you should somehow run out of fuel, there is a two-gallon can of gas in the trunk. That should get you to the next gas station."

"That's reassuring."

"If you get stopped, they'll probably search the car and find it. Just explain that you ran out of gas before and just wanted to be prepared. Be convincing! Hoarding is illegal. They'll probably take it from you anyway, though."

"Yes, I am sure they will."

"Finally, Sergio, let's talk about what you can do in case of a flat or a mechanical breakdown situation and anything else you want to discuss."

9 – Ford Deluxe

S alvador removed all traces of his existence in the bunkhouse. Before turning in that evening, he showered and packed a small suitcase that Raúl gave him with a change of underwear, pants, socks, and shirt.

"Thank you, Raúl. There's room in this suitcase for things Humberto is bringing me. You can keep the suitcase he brings in trade."

"I will probably get a better one from him," said Raúl, laughing.

That evening Salvador slept in one of the rocking chairs in Raúl's house to facilitate a quick and easy wakeup just before dawn.

A raucous wind-up alarm clock in Raúl's bedroom was so loud that it woke Salvador from a light sleep.

"You are awake. I hope you got some sleep, Sergio," said Raúl as he came into the living area. Salvador was already getting dressed.

"Oh yes! That alarm clock woke me up all the way out here. I'm surprised it doesn't have the rooster crowing an hour early in the dark."

"Humberto told me to feed you good this morning since you may not get to eat much today."

As Salvador tied his boots, he chuckled and said, "Yes, I am sure he's right."

"I'm hard-boiling two eggs for you. While I'm doing that, there's a loaf of bread in a cloth bag in the breadbasket. Take it with you. There are three slices of bread on the table to go with your eggs. Rice and beans will be ready in a minute too."

"Many thanks, Raúl. You are very kind."

"It's nothing! Have you thought of anything else you should take with you?"

"Yes, a full pot of that wonderful Cuban café con leche!" They both laughed.

The small suitcase Raúl had given Salvador sat beside the cloth bag containing bread by the front door. They waited anxiously in the two armchairs, chatting about nothing in particular, waiting for Humberto.

Not long after the windows showed the earliest evidence of the sun, shifting from a black sky to dark gray, a car drove up to the front of the house. Its headlights flashed the front window and went out. Salvador's excitement peaked. His heart skipped a beat. A brief shiver went through him. Recalling last night's final look at his makeshift calendar, he took a deep breath. Goodbye hiding place, hello God knows what. Another date for me to remember—Monday, August 27, 1962.

By the time Salvador walked to the door, Humberto was already on the porch with a suitcase.

With an expressionless face, Humberto nodded and said, "Good morning! Sergio, are you ready?"

"Ready!" said Salvador. "I'll quickly take the things in that suitcase and put them in this one Raúl gave me." After the item transfer was complete and the suitcases shut, he picked up the bread bag and looked at the car he would shortly drive away. Oh, look at that! 1940 Ford Deluxe 2-door. Just like dad's, only this one has a lot of rust and a faded paint job.

Humberto took a driver's license out of his sock, gave it to Salvador, and shook his hand. "I didn't want to get stopped with another person's license in my wallet or pocket. The keys are in the ignition. Second one on the ring is for the trunk. The gas tank is full. Registration is in the glove compartment."

"That's amazing," said Salvador, looking at his license.

"Put it in your wallet. You should know that we made it impossible to trace the car back to us. The VIN numbers have been obliterated or removed in all the places Ford puts them. That's not very unusual, so don't worry about that. But, although the license plate is as invalid as your license and registration, they are very convincing. The police or Army don't have a way to quickly check on those things. As long as they look valid, they will work."

Salvador took a deep breath. Yeah, unless I get arrested, and they have the time to find out. But I can't think about that. "That's all good to know, my friend. Thank you. I wondered about all this last night. I think I can fake my way through a document check."

"Good. Do you remember your route?" Humberto asked, looking at the folded map tucked under Salvador's waistband.

"Yes, I do."

"Do you want to take a look at the other map before you depart?"

"No, but thank you. I have that burned into my brain."

Humberto smiled, "Good luck, Sergio. Raúl will get me back home. Don't delay. Get moving. You have a long trip today."

Salvador extended his hand to Raúl, "Thank you for giving me a safe place to stay." He picked up his suitcase and turned to Humberto, "I have no words to thank you enough for what you have done. You and your people have done a miracle for me. Goodbye!"

"Come back and see us after we get rid of Fidel," said Raúl.

"Oh, don't think for a minute that I won't," Salvador called out over his shoulder as he walked briskly to the car, heart pounding with a mix of anxiety and happiness.

As Jefferson passed his secretary's desk, she handed him the special ops reading folder and his morning coffee. He sat down at his desk, took a quick sip, and opened the folder containing messages from the Operation Mongoose agents in Miami and several contacts of his own in multiple locations in the Caribbean. The message on top was from an informant in Cuba. He read it anxiously, then picked up his gray phone and dialed.

"Marv Jefferson here. Good morning. I have some news about your man."

"Let's have it," said Captain Patterson.

"It's a day old and short; they planned to give him a car this morning and send him to Gitmo. His ETA there is tomorrow evening if the wind don't blow too hard and the creek don't rise above the banks."

"We both know that isn't likely to go without a hitch. When will you know if it came off as planned this morning? Do you have any more details at all? I hope he was told about the minefields."

"Sorry, there are no more details. The earliest I could possibly get more word will be tomorrow morning. It's more likely that we'll know he's safe in Gitmo before I hear more from them. We have to trust that they thought of everything."

"Marv, that's hard to do."

"Faith, Dan, faith. Those guys are not amateurs. You have no idea."

Salvador took the keys from the ignition, opened the spacious trunk, put his suitcase in it, slid onto the torn tan cloth bench seat, and wound down both side windows. With a twist of the ignition key, the Ford Deluxe came to life. He put the old girl into first gear, gave her a little gas while releasing the clutch, and waved an adrenalin-trembling hand to Raúl and Humberto. Face flushed and ears burning, his meandering trek was underway to the closest U.S. soil, Naval Air Station, Guantanamo. He noted a slightly mellow tone to the engine, evidence of a small rust hole in the exhaust pipe or muffler. That's no problem. The windows will be open all the way. Unless it rains, then they will have to be cracked for air exchange. I've gotta calm down. I can do this. It's going to be OK.

The folded map was beside him, next to the bread bag. The image of the route to this evening's stopover was fresh in his mind. At least two fuel stops were needed before getting to Las Villas province. He wanted to enter that province with a full tank to get through it without stopping. Humberto told him there would be a significant amount of Cuban and Soviet activity at air bases and other military construction in the northern portion of Las Villas province. A limited amount of direct roads made it difficult to avoid military traffic since they served bases and other military construction sites. Therefore, his route was helter-skelter to avoid that traffic wherever possible.

Safely through Las Villas without being stopped, Salvador continued to frequently scan the rearview mirror. It was very loose and hard to keep at an angle to see out the rear window. Every significant bump in the road caused it to tilt downward. As he adjusted the mirror back into position after a rough patch of road, he saw an olive-drab jeep rounding a curve behind him. As it neared, giving him a better look, it appeared to be an old Soviet model, but the uniforms of the four men in it were clearly military. The jeep continued to catch up and then stayed behind him. His heartbeat quickened as time progressed, especially when they didn't pass him when the opportunities arose. *Oh shit. I can't tell if they are Army or police. When are they going to pull me over? There's a gas station. I have to stop. Here we go.*

He drove up to a gas pump and breathed a sigh of relief when the jeep passed by.

"Good morning, sir," said a teenage boy that came out of the quaint building that housed a small store. "Gasoline?"

"Yes, please."

"New here?" the boy asked as he watched the pump slowly tick off tenths of gallons.

"No. Passing through."

"Where are you going?"

"Visiting my grandmother in Cienfuegos."

"I love my grandmother. She lives with us and does most of the cooking."

"Grandmothers are the best cooks!"

The boy nodded with a smile in agreement, "She taught my mother, who is a good cook. They cook together." He stopped pumping just shy of three gallons and returned the nozzle to the pump receptacle. "Goodbye, sir."

"Goodbye, young man." *Now don't memorize my license number and report a stranger driving through. These stops are nerve-wracking.*

After several long and anxious hours, the day was coming to an end. He had unnervingly seen many Cuban and Soviet soldiers in jeeps and trucks in Matanzas province. The last of the bread had been eaten en

59

route. Thanks to successful stops, the fuel gauge was showing nearly three-fourths of a tank. With dusk close at hand, his planned overnight stop came into view on the outer edge of the south side of Victoria de las Tunas. It's just as Hubrto described it, one gas pump in front of 'Yaci's general store,' an old, two-story building.

A farmer's truck pulled away from the pump as Salvador came up to it. The gray-haired service attendant greeted him with a polite, monotoned, "Good evening, sir." Without further conversation, he removed the gas cap and pumped two gallons into the tank. When the gas cap was secured, he came to the driver's window and said, "You are ready to go, sir."

Salvador nodded, "Thank you, and good evening to you, sir! Do you know if I can get a loaf of bread in the store?"

"You will have to ask my wife inside."

"I am very tired. Can I park somewhere here and sleep in my car until sunrise?"

The man hesitated, then pointed, "Park over there. There's a hammock in the yard beside the store. As long as the breeze continues, the bugs will stay away."

"That's very kind, sir. Thank you."

Well, that's a blessing. Let's hope I can get some rest for tomorrow's ordeal. Now let's go see about tomorrow's bread.

Parked where instructed, he walked to the store. A lady that reminded him of his grandmother was fussing with a young boy behind the counter. "Good evening. Can I get a loaf of bread?"

"I can help you," the boy blurted out.

"Jorge, be quiet! Take your candy and go back home," she admonished.

Salvador chuckled and watched the boy scurry out the door.

She smiled, "My grandson is hard to control at times. Yes, sir, I do have one that's a day old. Will that be good?"

"Yes, thank you very much."

She wrapped a loaf of bread in a newspaper page and handed it to him.

The man he spoke to outside came into the store. "I told him he could sleep in the hammock tonight."

She nodded with an approving smile.

"Good evening to both of you. You are very kind." They seemed congenial. With luck, I won't be woken up by men in uniform.

With the bread placed on the car seat and the doors locked, he walked to the hammock in the very last of the sun's light and rolled into it. His tired body craved rest. His mind pushed away tension and began to play lovely tricks that allowed him to enjoy visions of Angela. Her voice rang clearly in his ears, her perfume was vivid, and the feel of her warmth beside him seemed real. The sandman quickly intervened, and he slipped into a guarded sleep.

Salvador woke before daybreak out of a subconscious fear of oversleeping, which could mean possibly driving the final miles in the dark. Meager light from a pole by the gas pump revealed a friendly white cat with brown paws and tail tip comfortably tucked upside down between his thighs. It turned over, stood, stretched with its back arched high, then jumped off the hammock and disappeared. Fidgeting for a more comfortable position, Salvador mentally rehearsed today's route plan while trying to conjure the sun's first light. The menacing visual of the final part of the trip rippled through his mind.

Oh, good grief! I think I'd rather walk on a bed of smoldering coals. He rolled and sat on the edge of the hammock. Oh, hell, I may as well sit in the car until there's enough light to get going. Let's see, it's Tuesday, the 28th of August. Gitmo, and those damn mines, here I come. He approached the driver's side of the car and smiled, seeing another newspaper-wrapped loaf of bread sitting on the running board.

"Good afternoon, Dan. How was your weekend?" Jefferson asked, settling back in his chair.

"Afternoon, Marv. It was good. The first long weekend I've had in a while. I took yesterday off too. First Monday off I've taken in a while. But we stayed home so I could be close to the phone. There's just too much going on right now. I needed the break, and I got caught up on my reading. How was your weekend?"

"Not as relaxing as yours. The only chance I get to read is when I'm on an airplane or in a hotel room. I could use a recommendation for my next trip."

"Ah, well, I just finished *Catch-22* by Joseph Heller and found it really good reading."

"Oh, I've heard of that one. A war novel. I'll pick up a copy. As for my weekend," he took a deep breath, "I was called in on both Saturday and Sunday for a while. But that's my normal life. You lead a charmed life, my friend. Mine keeps me single. No woman is willing to put up with it," he said with a laugh.

"Oh, sure, Marv. Mmhmm. I know you're not without, shall we say, female companionship. That Cheryl, who joined you and me for dinner a few times, is really something. She's smitten, too."

"Yeah, well, she tolerates me now and then," Jefferson said, chuckling. "We both have busy lives. Somehow, it has worked. It's been over three years now."

"It's more than that, Marv. She's a lovely lady."

"That she is."

"By the way, Marv, don't think I had all peace and pleasantries this weekend. I may have exaggerated a bit. OK! You have some news, I take it."

"Yes, I just got the word that your guy started his trip early yesterday morning. But that's all I have."

"Oh, thanks, Marv. I'll let our people in Gitmo know to expect him late this afternoon or evening, by the grace of God."

Salvador spotted two vacant pumps at a gas station on the northeastern outskirts of La Maya. He pulled up to one and got out to check his oil level. An attendant came to the pumps as Salvador was shutting the hood.

"Good morning, sir," the man said in a deep voice.

"Good morning, sir," Salvador replied as he leaned on the front fender.

A Cuban military truck pulled up on the other side of the pumps. "Fill this tank right away," the soldier in the truck's right seat barked at the attendant.

"Yes, Sergeant," the attendant said, leaving go of the nozzle in Salvador's tank and quickly going to the truck.

"We're looking for a missing soldier," said the Sergeant. "Do you know that man over there?" he asked the attendant, pointing at Salvador.

"No, Sergeant. Do you have a picture of the soldier you're looking for?"

"No, just his name and age, Lidio Desnoes, 29 years old."

Oh, shit. I know where this is going. Salvador felt an adrenalin rush and got back into the car. He turned the radio dial, ignoring the sound of the truck's door opening and shutting. Out of the corner of his eye, he saw a uniform coming around the gas pump to his car.

The Sergeant approached Salvador's open window and asked gruffly, "What's your name?"

Salvador looked up from the radio, "Sergio Lopez, Sergeant."

"Do you live in this area?"

"No, sir. I'm traveling to see my ill father and family in Los Reynaldos," said Salvador with every ounce of discipline he could muster to be calm.

"I want to see your driver's license and car registration!"

Oh, this guy isn't Army. He's militia or police. Salvador got the car's papers out of the glove compartment, then took his license out of his wallet.

The Sergeant grabbed them unceremoniously.

After examining Salvador's papers, the sergeant said, "Get out and open the trunk."

When he got out of the car and opened the trunk, Salvador noticed that the four soldiers in the back of the open stake truck had rifles, which he recognized as Czech R-2s, ready in both hands.

"Open the suitcase." The sergeant quickly searched through the contents. "What's in that can?"

"Gasoline, for the emergency of an empty tank."

The sergeant opened the gas can, took a brief smell, then held onto it. "Close the suitcase and the trunk. Get back in the car and be on your way."

Damn it, there goes my three-quarter tank safety net.

Salvador relived those moments of hearing that Sergeant's coarse voice at each of the two subsequent fuel stops. After finishing the last of a loaf of bread for a mid-morning snack while driving, he looked at his watch—11:47. Oh, this trip is going better than I thought. Making great time, maybe two hours to the air station gate and a little more than three-quarters of a tank, enough to make it all the way with plenty to spare.

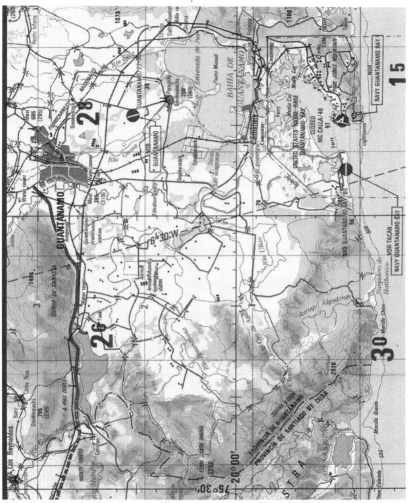

CIA, via Univ. Texas Libraries, https://creativecommons.org/about/cc0/

Joint Operations briefing map snip, US Navy lower right, plus action areas

10 – Close, But...

Huberto didn't mention this, Salvador whispered to himself, waiting fourth in a line of stopped vehicles. The holdup was due to major construction on a road he needed to cross northeast of Monte Prieto. He was behind a car that had two trucks in front of it. Drumming on the steering wheel with his fingers, he nervously watched the roadwork ahead. One truck was allowed to cross, raising his hopes. It seemed like hours before the next truck was allowed to cross. Referring to his watch, he grumbled under his breath. Good grief, at least twelve minutes wait for him. I could be here a half hour or more. To conserve fuel, he turned off the engine after moving up. At least they haven't been checking papers. I hope the only Cuban military present are the ones guarding those prisoners that are working. A few minutes later, both the truck and car ahead of him were allowed to cross. Salvador optimistically kept the engine running. He nervously watched the man controlling the crossing traffic, who called to someone and pointed at his car. That sent a chill to Salvador's gut. A man approached the traffic controller, speaking to him with authority while intermittently looking at the car. Wish I could hear that conversation. OK, Sal, calm down. Finally, he received the wave to cross. I'd damn sure like to know what that was all about.

Shortly after crossing, he came upon a small military convoy that was stopped at the bridge over Rio Majagua at Cabanas. He stopped thirty feet behind the last vehicle. It was a stake truck full of armed Soviet soldiers. Oh shit, Ruskies. I can't turn around. Wait it out. See what happens. I bet they're trying to figure out if the bridge will support that long flatbed truck with a huge crate on it.

A Soviet officer quick-stepped to Salvador's car, came to the window, and asked, "Вы говорите по-русски?"

"I don't understand," Salvador replied in Spanish.

The officer glared and spoke in heavily accented Spanish, "Where are you going?"

He recalled the name of a small village on the map further along his route, "El Suspiro."

"Why?"

"I am visiting my mother and father."

"How long have you been following us?"

"I haven't been following you. I just now crossed over that road construction back there and came up behind you."

The officer went to the back of the truck full of soldiers and had an inaudible conversation. He returned to the car and angrily ordered, "I want your papers and those for the car. The soldiers said you have been following them."

While he assembled the documents, his mind rambled, and adrenalin began raging through his body. Poor bastards told him what he wanted to hear out of fear. No sense in arguing with this guy. He handed the documents to the officer.

"Give me that map on the seat too. Get out of the car!"

Salvador's mind rambled during an uncomfortable blindfolded ride, with his hands and feet bound, in the back of the truck with the soldiers. He hoped they would talk among themselves to give some hints about something, anything. They spoke little for the rest of the trip to a Soviet base on the southern outskirts of Guantanamo city. There were sounds of construction equipment and activity. He was blissfully unaware that he was only about 15 miles north of his destination, the U.S. Naval Air Station at Guantanamo. Knowing this was a dire situation, he was attentive to anything the soldiers might say. Unknown to them, when they did begin talking while parked somewhere on the base, he understood all of it and learned where he had been taken—a Soviet missile base. He also learned that some soldiers were angry about having to lie about him following them. The KGB officer refused to believe what they saw and threatened consequences if they didn't change their stories.

Two soldiers carried him bodily into a smelly empty tent, then removed his blindfold and bindings. They left him without a word and zipped up the tent's front flap entrance. His watch was taken, and his pockets were emptied and pulled inside out. The voice of the officer that questioned him earlier ordered four men to guard all sides of the tent and shoot to kill if he attempted to escape. Drained from tension and the effects of adrenalin, he fell into a light drowsy sort of sleep.

He was awoken by a loud, angry Russian voice approaching.

"Lieutenant, why did you bring this Cuban and his car into my secret base?"

"Colonel Koskov, I know Cubans are not permitted. But he's not a worker. He was following our trucks and is suspicious. He needs to be interrogated," replied a Russian voice he recognized, walking quickly with the Colonel to the tent. The sound of their boots striking the ground hard was disturbing.

Oh, shit. This isn't going to be good. Act scared and innocent, Sal.

"You're new to this base, Lieutenant Travkin. Before you arrived today, you were told of its sensitivity and secrecy level. I am sure you searched him and his car thoroughly before you arrested him. Did you find weapons, cameras, or anything suspicious?"

"No, Colonel. I found nothing."

"Let's take a look at him. Does he speak Russian?"

"No, Colonel. I'll translate."

The tent's entrance flaps were unzipped and opened wide to allow light to flood in.

"Stay still!" the Lieutenant said to Salvador angrily. The Colonel and the Lieutenant looked in from the entrance.

"Ask him his name and why he was following our trucks," said the

Colonel, his eyes focused on Salvador.

"It was in my report, Colonel."

"I don't care what's in your report. Do what I ordered you to do. I want to see him answer."

"Yes, Colonel, I am sorry." The Lieutenant turned to Salvador. "Prisoner Lopez, why were you following our trucks?"

"Sir, I wasn't following your trucks. I had never seen your trucks until I got through the road construction a few miles behind you and had to stop when I got to the bridge where you were stopped."

The Lieutenant translated loosely for the Colonel.

"Ask him where he was going?"

"Prisoner Lopez, if you weren't following us, where were you going?"

"I was driving to El Suspiro to visit my mother and father."

After the Lieutenant translated his answer, the Colonel asked, "Did he tell you that when you questioned him on the road?"

"The Lieutenant's face flushed, "Yes, Colonel. But the soldiers in the rear truck said he was following us. So he is not telling the truth."

"How long were you stopped at the bridge?"

"About a half-hour."

"Why did you stop?"

"The senior convoy driver was inspecting the bridge because of the weight of the big truck. After that, he studied a manual, then made his recommendation to the convoy captain. That took a while."

"Where did the prisoner start following you?" asked the Colonel with sarcasm.

"I'm not sure. He was discovered at the bridge, as I described in my report," the Lieutenant said matter-of-factly.

"Where you were stopped and blocking traffic from getting around!

"Yes, Colonel."

"He's not lying. You're a fool for bringing him and his car onto this base. I will not have you on my base. Return to KGB headquarters in Havana tomorrow morning. Arrange for him to be turned over to the Cuban police. They can decide what to do with him. Be sure he's blindfolded and sees nothing before he leaves this tent."

"Yes, Colonel."

"Lieutenant, I want you and this prisoner off this base no later than 0900 hours tomorrow."

"Yes, Colonel," the Lieutenant said nervously, followed by a boot heel snap.

Salvador suffered a shiver like he had never experienced. His spine turned to ice, and his heart was racing. I am really in deep shit now. Oh, Angela, mom, dad—I hate the thought that I might not see you all again. C'mon, Sal, don't even think that. Saint Michael, look after me. Give me strength.

11 – Red in the Morning

Captain Daniel Patterson and Special Agent Marvin Jefferson had been nervously waiting since lunchtime in their respective offices for a call or message from Naval Air Station, Guantanamo. It was now 5:30. Petty Officer First Class Salvador Conte's safe arrival was becoming seriously doubtful.

Daniel could wait no longer. He dialed his secure phone. "Hey Marv, I'm biting my nails here! Anything from any of your many channels on my sailor?"

"Sorry, Dan. Not a peep. My timeline indicates that he should have gotten to NAS Gitmo well before 1600. He's run into trouble, but unfortunately, we don't know what or where. But I'm not leaving this office until I get some word from somebody. I asked my Operation Mongoose guys in Miami to probe their operatives in-country. I know you wanted to keep them out of this op. But this is getting critical."

"At this point, Marv, I totally agree. I just didn't want them involved earlier because I figured they'd find a way to use him as an asset there. But you're right. Getting out of our comfort zones is prudent."

"I understand! We now have, what is it you call it? A soup sandwich?"

"Aye. That it is. I've been worried about the Cuban and Marine mines around the Gitmo perimeter. If there's a mine explosion, will your people find out about it?"

"Probably. They've reported explosions and other base incidents in the past. I know what you're thinking. He ran into trouble, couldn't get to the base as planned, and tried getting to a gate or the fence elsewhere."

"Exactly. Was he briefed about the mines in his training there?"

"I am sure he was, but I'll check to make sure. But it probably focused on the gate areas. He's got a terrific memory, but Dan, we put a lot of things in his brain."

"Mmhmm, between you, NSA, and here, I'm worried about him being able to recall all that. Especially under duress."

"Dan, rest assured, if I hear anything at all regarding Conte or Gitmo, I'll let you know. But I can't expect timely reports from down there."

"OK, Marv, thanks. I'll try and get a message sent to the CO down there to add our command to reports of mine incidents until we get Conte safe. Gitmo isn't in our chain of command, so it will take some staffing and coordination to make that happen."

"Roger that. Alright, hang in there."

"I'll be in my office all night if need be. I'll check with Donnelly over at NSA to see if they've picked up anything that might be related."

Stirring and unintelligible distant voices outside woke Salvador from a light sleep. The sky seen through the small plastic windows in the tent's doors showed the first reddish-orange light of dawn. OK, this is Wednesday morning, August 29. It's getting harder to keep this straight. Red in the morning is a sailor's warning. This is gonna be a bad day. Even God is telling me that.

The sound of several pairs of heavy boots approaching the tent was unnerving. Here we go. It doesn't take that many to bring me breakfast, so they're gonna haul my sorry ass off to the Cubans.

"Tie his hands and feet, put on a blindfold, and get him into the truck," the Soviet Lieutenant barked angrily.

He's back! He should be angry at his own dumb ass, not me. If he had just let me go around that convoy, I would be safe in Gitmo, and he'd still have a career in the KGB.

Two soldiers untied the tent doors, entered the tent, and secured ropes tightly around Salvador's hands and feet. One of them tied a foul smelling rag around his eyes.

My Italian skin doesn't need any more oil, especially old engine oil.

Damn, that rag stinks.

Salvador spent what he guessed was twenty to thirty minutes bound and blindfolded, on his side, in the flatbed of a truck, being jolted from bumpy roads. Keeping your neck stiff to keep your head from banging on the floor was difficult. The bigger bumps in the road were doubly painful. When the truck had stopped, his anxiety heightened.

A truck door opened and closed. The Soviet soldier that got out asked someone, "Do you speak Russian?"

"No hablo ruso. Un momento."

Well, that tells me I'm about to be turned over to Cubans. This is going to take everything I've got. God, you need to help me!

Time dragged by until they found someone that spoke Russian.

"We received a call from your base. We will accept your prisoner," a Sergeant said in Russian with a heavy Cuban accent. "Do you have his papers?"

"No papers, just him, sir," said the Soviet soldier.

"Why do you bring me a prisoner without any papers?"

"They didn't give me any papers, Sergeant."

"Cut him loose and get him down. I'll call your base about the papers."

A Soviet soldier ripped off the blindfold, threw it on the truck bed, and pointed at two Soviet soldiers with AK-47s pointed at Salvador.

The Cuban looked at Salvador and said, "Don't talk or fight, or they will shoot."

"Salvador nodded, allowing his fear to show, hoping to make a good impression of innocence.

Two quick slices of a sharp combat knife freed his hands and feet. The soldier stood back and motioned with his weapon for Salvador to get off the truck.

Four Cuban soldiers with pistols drawn waited for him at the gate of a chain-linked fence around a building. One wore Sergeant insignia. A sign on the gate read words to the effect that it was the Headquarters of the Guantanamo Ministry of the Interior Provincial Police.

Salvador looked at the men inside and outside of the fence around their HQ. That CIA briefer was right. Their police dress in the same uniforms as the Army.

The moment Salvador's shoes hit the ground, Cuban soldiers handcuffed him.

"Don't make any quick moves," said the Sergeant. "You are under arrest."

"Yes, Sergeant. I don't know why the Soviets arrested me. All I did was…"

The Sergeant interrupted him, "Don't talk unless you are asked a question." He nodded at two soldiers standing by and motioned at the building. "Get him into a cell."

The soldiers grabbed Salvador under the arms and hauled him through the gate, his feet sometimes dragging the ground. He allowed himself to shake somewhat uncontrollably, again hoping to show innocence. They took him through double doors, along a hallway, down a flight of stairs, and shoved him forcefully into a cell. There were eight cells in their musty, foul smelling dungeon. Four in a row on each opposing side of the room. Only one was empty until now.

The clank of the barred door behind him and the metallic snap of the lock sent ice water into his bloodstream.

This is lovely, he thought as he picked himself up from a concrete floor-level close-up view of a flimsy, odd-smelling, and grossly stained pillow. I have no blanket, no bed, not even a mattress. The window is boarded, so no fresh air. Just f'n lovely!

He looked over to the rusty galvanized bucket in the corner that was discolored and wreaking a sickening stench. That thing's probably never been anything but emptied. And I thought I had seen the worst. At least there are cracks between the boards in the window. I'll be able to keep track of days.

Pacing, with his mind reeling in freefall, he tried fighting off intense sensations of anxiety, skin prickling, and the churning in his gut. He sat down with his back to the wall, facing the door, closed his eyes, and attempted to will his hands to stop trembling. I sure hope DC knows where I am, somehow. Even so, how will they get me out of this mess? Don't think like that, Sal. Keep the faith. They said always have faith. With his knees pulled up, his arms wrapped around them, and his forehead resting on his knees, he tried to find some semblance of peace. Vivid snippets of myriad events from the last few months wandered and danced through his troubled mind. Vignettes of Angela and his mother and father were interspersed with flashes of many and varied visions from the recent past. The torment of it all was too great to let continue. He opened his eyes and put a stop to those painful thoughts.

"Get up and take all your clothes off. Everything!" barked a man outside the bars in fatigues, officer insignia, and his hand on a holstered Colt 45. A soldier with a Russian PPSh-41 submachine gun was at the officer's side.

"Yes, sir," was the best answer he could muster, taking off his clothes and piling them up in front of him. Time to show a lot of fear and vulnerability again. He made himself start trembling, which took little effort, given the circumstances.

"Give me your gun and search all his clothes!" the officer ordered the soldier. "Mr. Lopez, kick those clothes toward the door, move to the corner by the bucket, face the corner, and don't move."

"Yes, sir." As if I'm going to try something with a weapon that could tear me apart pointed straight at me. Salvador watched the man squeeze all his clothes, looking for something in the pockets or sewn into seams.

The soldier looked back toward the officer. "Nothing, Lieutenant."

"Come get your gun and keep an eye on him," said the Lieutenant. "Mr. Lopez, turn around slowly, then put your clothes on."

When his clothes were back on, he was handcuffed and taken out of the prison room to a nearly empty room with only a small square-topped wooden table with two chairs on opposing sides.

"Stand behind that chair!" the soldier ordered. His menacing submachine gun remained pointed at Salvador.

The Lieutenant entered the room, sat across from Salvador, and promptly began his questioning. "The Soviet base told me you said your name is Sergio Lopez, but you had no papers. How do I know that's who you are?

"Yes, I said that! But it was confirmed on the driver's license and car registration they took from me," Salvador said in a contrived, lightly trembling voice.

The Lieutenant's eyebrows twitched. He opened the middle drawer of the table, took out a pad and pencil, and began taking notes. "Car? You were driving a car?"

"Yes, Lieutenant," Salvador said. He continued with an explanation of the details about coming upon the Soviet convoy and the subsequent arrest. The Lieutenant took copious notes.

Taking a moment to absorb all that, the Lieutenant put the pencil down, clasped his hands, and rolled his thumbs. "Mr. Lopez, your story is very different from the one I have received." He studied Salvador's face intently.

"I have told you the truth of what happened, Lieutenant."

"I think you're lying. Where were you going?"

"I was driving to El Suspiro."

"Why?"

"To visit my mother and father. It's been almost two years since I've seen them. Since I left home at 17, I have tried to visit them as often as I can."

"Why are you so nervous?"

"I have never been arrested! I have never done anything wrong!"

The Lieutenant peered into Salvador's eyes without expression but with a cold penetrating stare. "What have you been doing since leaving home?"

"I did many odd jobs while working my way to Havana. I heard such wonderful things about it. When I saved enough money working in Havana, I went to Miami." *That will help explain any American accent I have. I've got to keep these lies straight in my head. They need to be close to what I told Dr. Basilio and that Soviet Major.*

"When did you come back to Cuba?"

"It was about October or November 1958."

"What were you doing in Miami during that time?"

"Oh, I worked at the docks in Miami as a mechanic's helper. I saw all those cruise ships and merchant ships coming and going and got the urge to travel. It wasn't long before I found a job on a freighter from Barcelona. I worked on that ship until it came to Havana for the first time. I left the ship then so I could be back home in my Cuba."

"When did you come back to Havana?"

"About two years ago." *A shiver went through him. This guy is going to catch me in a lie, sooner or later.*

"What month was it?"

"I don't remember the exact month. It might have been July or August. It was during summer and before cane harvest."

"What was the name of the ship you were on?"

"Banderos II."

"What work did you do on the Banderos?"

"I was a helper in the Engineering Department. I learned a lot about engines and electrical work aboard her. I also learned to defend myself too." He faked a small chuckle. *I hope they can't check that ship's name or any of this bullshit anytime soon. At least long enough to give Marv Jefferson and Captain Patterson a chance to get my ass out of here. They better hurry. It probably won't take them too long to find out there's no Sergio Lopez and Banderos never docked in Havana.*

The Lieutenant took notes, frequently pausing to look into Salvador's eyes sternly. When he stopped writing, he looked up. "Where are you living now?"

"I'm not living anywhere, Lieutenant. I was coming to this area to look for a new place to live. I last worked for an auto repair garage in Camilo Cienfuegos, near Santa Cruz. I boarded there for a while and left to return to this area."

"Who boarded you there?"

"A fine man named Tomas Alvarez and his wife, Dalita. You won't find any two more loyal to Fidel Castro and the revolution than they are. I owe them a lot."

"What did the Soviet base do with your car?"

"I don't know. I haven't seen it since the day they arrested me."

"Where did you get the pesos to buy it?"

"I saved a lot of money working on the ship. I bought the car from a man in Havana."

"When was that?"

"It was probably around October or November 1958."

"What kind of car was it?"

"A 1940 Ford Deluxe."

"What color?"

"Black."

"What was the license number?"

"Um, I'm sorry, Lieutenant, I can't remember. I never memorized it."

After jotting down information about the car, the Lieutenant paused, staring at Salvador. "If you got your car back, what would you do with

77

it?"

Now, that's a strange question. Let's try this. "I'll probably live in it until I find a place to board."

What a cold bastard! Not the slightest reaction. He is definitely real trouble for me. No sense of humor. I need to use that damn bucket before I piss my pants.

The Lieutenant reviewed his notes, then looked up and stared at Salvador.

Oh my God, stop boring into my brain. Just ask a damn question!

Finally breaking his stare, the Lieutenant motioned to the soldier, "Take this prisoner back to his cell."

It was difficult for Salvador to keep from looking at the vertical slices of light between the boards in the window. It helped take his mind from pangs of hunger and thirst. He sat on the concrete floor, back against the wall, and watched spears of light being cast from the window. The rays moved slowly across the cell floor and up onto the bars.

Oh, the window faces west. This day is coming to an end. I haven't seen food for anyone all day. I'm so hungry it's making me feel sick.

A soldier sat at the table in the room's center with what he recognized as a Czech VZ-23 submachine gun lying on the table. He spent the day smoking cigars and cigarettes, scanning the cells, and stretching now and then. Salvador ignored him because otherwise, the result was an angry glare in return.

The guard stood when two soldiers entered with trays of small bowls and paper cups. "Remain away from the cell doors until your food is placed inside," he barked loudly.

Salvador watched a meager excuse for food get placed through bars onto cell floors on the other side of the room. He watched in envy as the man in the cell across from him devoured the contents of the bowl and emptied a paper cup of water in fast gulps.

A few moments later, the soldiers returned with the same haute cuisine for Salvador's side of the room. As soon as the soldier left his cell door, he drank the thin, bland oatmeal sort of gruel from the small bowl. Dried residue from many previous uses was evident on the sides and rim. Swigging water from a paper cup that had surely been used many times before did not sate his thirst. Hmm, I wonder if I can order seconds, thirds, maybe. He smiled at his fleeting moment of gallows humor.

The guard yelled, "Put your bowls and cups by the door and move to the rear wall."

Oh, this is when nattily dressed busboys will clear our tables. This is a class restaurant I'll be sure to recommend to others.

Two soldiers reached through each cell's bars to collect the bowls and cups and departed.

Sitting with his back to the wall, knees up, and his hands clasped around them, he closed his eyes and conjured up an image of a peaceful lake while his stomach growled in protest. He wondered when and how that horribly foul smelling bucket would get emptied.

12 – That Damn Car

S alvador woke, rolled onto his back, and stretched a multitude of aching muscles.

Oh joy! Early morning of my second full day here in lovely Guantanamo. So close to the Navy, yet so far. Yesterday was hard to take. I better get used to this. There's no telling how long the starvation diet and interrogations will last. Let's see, this is Friday morning, August 31st. I wonder what wonderful events will unfold. Good grief, why am I making humor out of this.

The guard at the center table stood when a soldier entered the jail area with a drawn pistol. "Pick up your buckets and wait by your cell door."

One prisoner at a time walked slowly to the far end of the jail with a pistol at their back. They were then ordered to turn on a spigot and empty their buckets into a drain hole in the floor. A broom was leaning against the wall to be used for sweeping any remaining contents into the drain.

Bracing for his grisly turn, Salvador reached into his core to find the mental discipline to endure this day. I guess there's nothing like a little hard labor to work up a good appetite for breakfast.

"Make it quick, gentlemen," JFK said, hands clasped on the resolute desk in the Oval Office. "The helo is on its way. I'm going to Newport."

Standing in front of the desk was Dean Rusk, Secretary of State, and McGeorge Bundy, National Security Advisor to the President.

Rusk began the conversation, "Mr. President, I felt I should come in with Mac when he briefed you on the latest Cuban intelligence. You may want me to take some diplomatic action, and I know you're on a tight schedule to get to Rhode Island and will be out of Washington for a few days."

Taking Rusk's nod, Bundy cleared his throat. "Mr. President, in a nutshell, analysis of films from an August 29 U-2 reconnaissance flight confirms without question that there are several surface-to-air missile installations in Cuba, and they are operational. Collateral intelligence indicates that they are there to protect the expanding Cuban Air Bases and the Soviet bases being constructed in several locations, as previously briefed. The evidence is becoming progressively more certain that the Soviets are rapidly constructing intermediate and medium-range ballistic missile sites. We have also confirmed the presence of anti-ship SSM, surface-to-surface mobile missile launchers at several locations."

"We haven't confirmed, beyond doubt, that ballistic missiles are there, correct?" asked JFK.

"Correct, but…"

JFK interrupted, "Will this preclude the U-2 missions over Cuba?"

"No, Mr. President," Bundy said emphatically. "U-2s can fly higher than their anti-aircraft missiles can reach and give us good photography. The Soviets and Cubans can't do a thing against a U-2."

"I don't plan to authorize any air or naval strikes on Cuba, so my interest lies solely in the ballistic missiles. It's frustrating, gentlemen, but continue to keep a lid on this until I can nail Khrushchev with undeniable evidence. They are still denying offensive weapons are there, correct Dean?"

"Yes, Mr. President, at all military and political levels," said Rusk.

"This is troublesome and one hell of a quandary," said JFK, shaking his head. "But for now, we will take no diplomatic or military actions or leak what we know they're up to. However, Mac, the second you know for certain that there are ballistic missiles of any kind there, I want to know, right then, day or night. We can't get caught with our proverbial pants down."

"Captain Patterson!" Dan replied into his secure phone.

"It's Marv Jefferson, Dan. I just got word from the Op Mongoose boys in Miami. Conte is being held at the Cuban police HQ in Guantanamo. He almost made it, Dan."

"Damn. Close does not count a damn bit. Glad you caught me. I was getting ready to go get some dinner. That's news I wouldn't want to have missed for an hour or so. What now, Marv?"

"Good question, Dan. I'm trying to figure out if there's any possibility of springing him. I'm going to take a look at the photography we've got on that building. My guess is that it's heavily protected, so our only chance would be if they move him. That would mean a capture team would have to be watching that building and be ready to act 24/7. That would be a difficult thing to ask them to do. But I'll ask the Mongoose guys what they think. Go get dinner. I'll give you a ring later. I'll take a thorough look at the images and have a heart-to-heart with the boys in Miami."

"OK, Marv. I'll grab something quick and get back in the office. I'll be here like I said until things get resolved in some manner."

"Take your time. This will take me a couple hours or so."

Three days later, Salvador woke to a new day and began his morning regimen of bucket tending, stretching, jumping jacks, pushups, and situps. While walking in place, cooling down, exhausted from hunger, his mind wandered.

OK, it's Monday, September 3, my fifth day in this pig sty. C'mon, DC, it's a work day, so get to work. Make something happen.

He passed time by pacing his cell like a big cat in a zoo cage. It made the guard at the desk watch him like a taunted zookeeper. I'd holler, boo! But he'd jump and get pissed off. Then tell that damn Lieutenant some lie so I'd get some ungodly damn punishment. It would be fun, though. Stop it, Sal; think about mom, dad, and Angela.

The angles of sunbeams piercing the gaps in the window boards were

Salvador's sundial. The morning had slipped by during oblivion. Salvador realized the sunbeams were indicating it was now a little after noon. The sound of the jail room's heavy door opening and shutting was followed by the appearance at his cell door of a soldier.

Ah, the Lieutenant's lackey is here to escort me to another round of talks. This should be interesting.

Salvador's cell was opened without a word, just motions from the soldier. Hands cuffed in front, he was hustled away for questioning.

"Stand behind the chair at attention," the soldier ordered gruffly and went to a corner by the door of the questioning room.

Several minutes later, the cold, calculating Lieutenant entered, put a pad and pencil on the desk, scowled, and in a surprising move, punched Salvador in the gut hard. "Mr. Lopez, why did you lie to me about having a car?"

Doubled over, nearly collapsing, Salvador fought for his breath.

"Stand up when I talk to you!"

Still gasping, standing straight up was impossible, but he did the best he could. Finally able to speak, he managed to say, "Lieutenant, I swear... on my mother's grave... I was driving... when the Soviets... arrested me."

"The Soviet base commander insists you were arrested snooping around their base on foot."

I have nothing to lose here. I need to at least create doubt in his mind. "Lieutenant, they just want my car. Giving you the car and its papers would result in losing face for lying. I have told you the truth!" I can't believe he lets me talk so much.

The Lieutenant reached into his pocket and put Salvador's driver's license on the table. "The Soviets said they misplaced this and sent it over to me but said that is all they have. I checked your license with Havana, and it is valid. So, you didn't lie about being Sergio Lopez."

Salvador nodded calmly, naturally. Good grief, Humberto's contacts are good. They must have a hell of a network of people in the right places.

"But, you are still lying because Havana has no record of a car in your name. You're lying about the car. You will be charged with lying."

"I'm not lying, Lieutenant. If you put someone outside their base, you'll see my car, a black 1940 Ford Deluxe coupe. There's a rusted dent just below the gas cap, and the rearview mirror is loose and won't stay in position. I was taken there in a Soviet truck blindfolded and brought to you blindfolded in a Soviet truck. How could I possibly know those things?" Oh, that made his eyebrows move. I think a lightbulb just came on.

Another unexpected powerful punch in the gut sent Salvador to the floor. He writhed on the floor in pain, fought off tunnel vision, and tried to catch more than slight breaths.

"Get up! Stand at attention!" shouted the Lieutenant. "Don't insult our Soviet friends!"

Disabling pain eased enough for Salvador to finally take gulps of air. He managed on the second attempt to stand, but clumsily. Damn, this hurts. I wish they had closed that registration loophole.

"The truth now, liar!"

"Lieutenant, I think the reason there's no car record… I bought the car from a man who sold them at the docks. He came there and sold cars and other things during our noon breaks. I gave him pesos, and he came back with car papers and keys. He made it easy for the dock workers to get things done. It was hard to get time off. Many of us bought and sold cars through him. If he gave me invalid papers, how was I to know? They looked real to me." Look at his face. He doesn't know whether to believe me or not, and he has no way of checking my story. That damn car is going to be the reason I don't get out of this.

The Lieutenant sat down and crossed his arms for a moment. "Tell me again, everything about when the Soviets arrested you." He took fresh notes as Salvador again described in detail how he was detained at the road construction, with no military convoy in sight, then came upon the Soviet convoy stopped at the bridge.

Striking a contemplative look with unflinching eye contact for a moment, the Lieutenant said, "I still think you're lying!. Are you a conspirator against our government?"

"No, Lieutenant. I am not and never have been."

"I know who you are, but I don't know what you are. I will find out if your mother and father exist, as you say. I will find out if all the parts of your story are true." He sat back and stared at Salvador.

I'm not going to let that damn Lieutenant stare me down. Don't blink, Sal.

The Lieutenant broke his stare in a few moments, looked over at the soldier, and ordered, "Put this criminal back in his cell!"

"Good afternoon, Dan. The Mongoose boys have done some serious thinking about your sailor. I also discussed the situation in detail with my boss. I'm sorry, but the bottom line is that we need a plan B, and I don't have one."

Captain Patterson's heart skipped a beat. "I suspected that's where we'd wind up. Damn it! I've been wracking my brain. I've got nothing, but I'll keep thinking."

"Roger that. Me too. Let's see what develops. If they wind up buying his story, whatever that might be, they'll let him go. All he has to do then is find his way to the Naval Station. But if they decide he's guilty, they may choose to try, convict, and kill him. If he's the luckiest son of a bitch alive, they do what they've done in the past. That is, hold him hostage for someone or, more likely, some assets we have frozen here. Otherwise, his luck has run out, and there's not a damn thing we can do about it."

Dan sighed, "You were doing good until that otherwise part, Marv."

"I know. It's hard to swallow. But I'm not giving up. I'm still working on it. Your man wouldn't be the first we've pulled out of there against terrible odds." He hung up the phone and paused. Poor bastard, I think, in this case, Conte's got as much chance as a snowball in hell."

13 – Now What?

Salvador woke from a deep sleep from the sound of an aluminum food bowl hitting the floor of his cell. He went to the bowl and devoured the bland and measly breakfast gruel.

I don't know if I can last a third day of hard work 'til dark in leg chains. The blisters on my hands have blisters. OK, Sal, calm down; think of it as a day out of this jail. Let's see, this is Thursday, September 6th. That makes it, uh, eight days in here. Come on, DC, make something happen. Patience! I need to be tough. Good grief, I never thought I'd want to be left alone all day in this stinking cell. It would damn sure beat a hard labor detail in the hot sun with no food. At least they gave us a canteen of water and refilled it. It would be nice if they'd at least hose me down before they bring me back to my cell. Oh, my God, these assholes are brutal. But I can't let them get to me.

It wasn't long before four soldiers came into the jail. Two came to Salvador's cell, and two went to another prisoner's cell.

"Stand up, put your hands behind your back, and turn around," a soldier ordered. "It is time to do some more work for Cuba! Do not talk unless a soldier talks to you. Do not talk to other workers."

Salvador nodded and complied. When leg irons and handcuffs were secured, he was taken to an old pickup truck with the other prisoner. They were lifted roughly into the truck bed and were chained to rings welded onto the sides.

When the truck arrived at the construction site, Salvador and the other prisoner, a gaunt and demoralized young man, possibly in his early twenties, were uncuffed and put to work. Strenuous work—taking bricks off the back of a truck bed, filling a wheelbarrow, and getting them to the bricklayers. Pushing a wheelbarrow over soft ground while still in leg irons that allowed only short shuffling strides was just short of cruel. So he loaded as few bricks as he could get away with.

Salvador dug deep into his core to mitigate the pain that set afire the blisters on his hands and the muscles of his legs and arms. His mind focused on ignoring the pain as he filled the umpteenth wheelbarrow with only as many bricks as he could get away with. The soldiers watched to make sure prisoners weren't slacking.

While returning to the truck for another load, he let his mind wander. Oh, thank you, mother nature, for this overcast day. Now bless us with some light rain. While you're at it, bless these bricklayers so they can finish this damn building quickly.

Two canteens of water later, and with only a brief rain shower late in the afternoon, sunlight was finally disappearing. Salvador was teetering at total exhaustion. Darkness couldn't come soon enough.

"Go to the back of the pickup truck!" the soldier barked.

Salvador and his jailmate couldn't shuffle to the truck fast enough.

Oh, finally, the torture is over. The kid looks white. I think they're going to kill him. I'll bet corporal asshole never worked ten minutes this hard in his life.

Hands cuffed and chained to the truck sides, the two jailbirds cat-napped during their trip back to their luxury suites, anxious for a great meal and a good night's rest. Despite the bumps and jolts, which sent pain from the pelvis up the spine of the two aching men, they still managed to drift off intermittently.

Suddenly there was a short clatter of gunfire. The truck swerved and lurched into a ditch, came abruptly to a stop, and tilted to one side. When

Salvador came to his senses after the violent jolt, he saw, through the hazy light of a three-fourths moon, several armed civilians approaching the truck from the woods on both sides of the dirt road. The two soldiers in the front of the pickup truck were not trying to get out or use their weapons. Steam was gushing out of the front of the truck and rose listlessly into the air. Two attackers dragged the lifeless bodies of the two soldiers out of the truck, put a single shot into their heads, and left them lying in the ditch.

A man with bolt cutters came to the rear of the truck, climbed up into the bed, and said, "We will free you and take you to safety."

Holy shit, I can't believe what just happened. I don't know who these guys are, but I have nothing to lose. "Many thanks, sir!"

Another man freed Salvador's jailmate and whisked him off.

Riding in the bread truck was a beautifully cruel punishment. The smell of bread remained from the day's cargo. Although drained of strength, Salvador drooled for the first time in many days.

"Why were you in jail?" the driver asked.

"I was driving my car and came to a Soviet convoy stopped at a bridge. They arrested me for no reason, then turned me over to the Ministry of Interior Police. I was accused by the Soviets of snooping their base, which was a lie."

"What's your name?"

"Sergio."

"Full name."

"Sergio Lopez."

"You don't sound like you are from this area."

"I'm not. It's a long story."

"Where would you like me to let you out?"

"I have no idea. I'm not from this area. No matter where I get out, wandering around looking like this, I'll get reported to the militia and get put back in prison."

"Did you have any identification when they arrested you?"

"I did, but the Soviets took it and gave it to the police. They verified my driver's license. They even showed it to me, so I know the police have it. But they had a problem verifying my car's registration. I must have bought it from an unreliable person, who gave me invalid papers. The police didn't believe me."

"They don't believe anything we say. I don't know who you are, Sergio, but I think you are worth rescuing."

"Yes, sir. Believe me, I am. Very much so."

That was the last of their conversation for another half hour.

"We have arrived," said the driver after a twenty-minute ride.

"Hallelujah! Where are we?" asked Salvador but got no reply.

After parking the truck in the dimly lit garage side of a bakery, the driver said, "Don't get out until I close the garage door."

"I'll wait right here," Salvador said with a chuckle that hurt. Thank you, Washington, if this is your doing. I can't believe this has happened.

The rescuer opened the truck's passenger door, "Are you able to walk?"

"Yes, sir. I hurt all over, but I can walk."

"On the other side of that wall is my bakery. My house is in back of this building. You need a shower and some clean clothes. Then some food and water. Then I am sure you will want to sleep."

"That will be wonderful, sir." He didn't bring me here to turn me in, so I have to trust him. I just wonder what price I'll have to pay and how.

"Follow me. My name is Cheche."

"I cannot thank you as much as you deserve." He's only giving me his nickname. I don't blame him. I might have to trust this guy now, but I must be careful what I tell him. He's got to be in cahoots with the government to be the village baker. But I have no choice. We'll just have to let this play out. I'll either be reported, discovered, or taken somewhere else. Holy shit, when does this adventure end?

Salvador followed Cheche out the warehouse's back door, across a small yard, and into the home's rear door. Standing two steps into the hallway was his first look at Cheche in good light. He's about 5'6", 40s, and in good physical shape, starting to get gray already. Looks like a pretty decent house. Comforting and disconcerting too. He's doing well, and that could be a problem.

A woman entered the hallway. "This is my wife, China," he said, turning to his wife, "This is Sergio. He'll be staying with us for a short time."

She looked surprised. "Nice to meet you," she said without emotion.

Salvador hid his own surprise. Oh, short time. OK, but what's next. She's not happy about this. I need to be careful. "Nice to meet you, China. Thank you for your hospitality."

"It's nothing," she said, still showing no pleasure in the situation.

"I'll go away while you get him clean," she said and left the hall.

She's really short, can't be more than 5'2". In her 30s. Beautiful long brown hair like Angelina.

Cheche pointed at the floor, "Take off all your clothes and drop them right there. I'll take them out and burn them while you're getting shaved and showered. You can use my straight razor."

Sergio couldn't get out of his grungy clothes fast enough.

"OK, follow me to the bathroom. I'll get a towel and some clothes. They'll be on the toilet lid by the time you're done showering."

"I can't tell you how good that's going to feel. Thank you!"

Clean for the first time in too many days and in clothes that had the uniquely pleasant smell from being dried on a line outdoors, he felt like a human being again. Salvador went to where he heard Cheche and China talking. "I could smell food cooking while I was getting dressed," Salvador said, entering the kitchen.

"Have a seat, Sergio. She almost has it ready."

Salvador sat at the four-place table on one end of the kitchen. A white demitasse cup of coffee sat patiently on its saucer, waiting for him. Café Cubano had always been more flavorful than what he was used to in the Navy. The first sips of it lit his taste buds, as usual, and put a smile on his face. "Oh, that is so good, thank you! I really need this!" Maybe he's alright since he has coffee, he joked to himself.

Watching China put chicken and fried plantains on three plates put Salvador's salivary glands in overdrive. When she put his plate down in front of him, Sergio said, "Heavenly! This just smells heavenly. You don't know how long since I had a decent meal."

"I can guess, Sergio. It all came from our garden, except the chicken. That's a little of our ration for the week."

China went back to get her plate and sat down. Salvador wanted badly to dive in but restrained himself, which took all the discipline he could muster. Cheche said grace for the food and added, "God bless Cuba."

Salvador used even more control from within to pace his eating with theirs. Their plates had equal amounts of everything; although Salvador had two chicken wings, they each had a drumstick.

When they had finished their plates, Salvador said, "I'm so grateful for what you are doing for me."

"Cafecitos, Cheche?" China asked.

"Yes, please." Cheche took a deep breath and turned to Salvador, "My friends and I have done many things for our cause since Castro took over and brought communism to Cuba. They have taken everything and made our lives worse. They are ruining our wonderful country. One day soon, we hope, they will be removed from power."

Salvador nodded. What dare I say? "Well, I'm glad one of those things you are doing is rescuing prisoners. Especially me."

"You are not the first that we have rescued. Some have turned out to be criminals that should have stayed in prison. I don't think you are one of those, or I would have put you out to wander on foot somewhere."

"Sir, you can be certain that I don't belong in their prison."

China finished making the deliciously sweet, thick, and strong cafecitos and brought them to the table. She remained quiet as they finished their dessert coffees. Salvador and Cheche chatted about Salvador's arrest experiences.

After clearing the table, she washed all the dinnerware and walked behind Cheche, still sitting at the table with Salvador. She put her hands on his shoulders, "I'm very tired, Cheche. I'm going to bed."

"Good night, my love. I won't be up much longer," he said, putting his hand on top of hers. Cheche looked Salvador in the eye, smiling briefly. "You told me about how you got arrested. Tell me about you, what you do, where exactly were you going when they arrested you?"

Hmm, he suspects there's something more going on. What should I say? Shall I spill the beans now or wait for some other time when my gut tells me? Salvador gave Cheche the cover story he created for the police.

After digesting all that, Cheche said, "Your time spent in Miami and on that merchant ship might explain your accent. I'll arrange to get you to your parent's house tomorrow."

Oh, shit. He's a clever fisherman. It's gotta come out now. "Cheche, I am sorry for not being completely honest. Where I am trying to go is the Navy Base in Guantanamo."

The surprise on Cheche's face was unmistakable. He stared at Sergio a moment, then the sides of his mouth turned slightly up. "I had a feeling you were an American. I won't ask any more questions. I will do what I can to help you. My friends and I helped a man get into the Navy Base about two years ago. It will not be easy for you or us, and it will take some time to plan and organize. For now, we should get some rest. You'll be in my son's old bedroom. It is small, but you will be more comfortable than you were in that prison cell."

14 – The Plan

Asharp thunderclap and the sound of heavy rain beginning to beat on his bedroom window woke Salvador. He rolled over, sat on the edge of the bed with his feet on the wood plank floor, and stretched. The humidity was so high he could taste and smell it.

I'm glad I shut that window last night when it was just light rain. I sure hope this storm isn't an omen of things to come. Let's see, my mental calendar says it's Friday morning, September 7. I'd think this was a dream if I didn't know better. It's quiet out there. Wonder what time it is? I can't wait any longer; I need to use the head.

"Good morning, Sergio," Cheche said as they met in the hallway.

"Good morning, Cheche. I hope I didn't wake you."

"No, we are usually up at sunrise, but today the sky was dark. The thunder and lightning woke us. I'll meet you in the kitchen."

Jefferson's secure phone rang, jolting him from concentrating on a document. "Good morning, Dan."

"How'd you know it was me?" asked Captain Patterson, pushing back from his desk in OP-20-G."

"I looked at the clock—0810. You're a man of strict habit," Jefferson said with a chuckle. " Before you ask, I haven't heard anything from my contacts in-country or the Mongoose boys in Miami. Beyond what we previously heard about him being imprisoned in Guantanamo City, I've heard not one damn thing."

"Would you know if they transferred him up the chain or tried him in some court?"

"That would all depend on so many things. It's hard to say."

"What do you think about getting the Department of State involved?"

"To negotiate his release?"

"Affirmative!"

"That would confirm him to be a high-value asset of some sort, thus guilty of several crimes, in their eyes. Frankly, Dan, given what's going on down there right now, I don't think we can afford to compromise him and create the storm that would follow."

"Damn it, Marv, at some point, we're going to have to go some extra mile to save that guy's ass."

"I hear your angst; I really do. But my experience is telling me that now is just not that time."

"I hate like hell to tell the Admiral where we're at right now, which is nowhere. Doing nothing is just not how I'm built, or the Admiral either, for that matter. He likes to hear solutions to problems. We have none."

"Sorry to say, right now, you're right. None. We just have to let this play out."

"Living in this building 24/7, waiting for some word, is getting old."

"Patience, my friend, patience. I'm in the same boat. Our people, and our informants down there, are much more clever than you or I can imagine."

"I can only hope and pray, Marv."

Salvador sat back from the breakfast table, sipping the dregs of his coffee.

China turned to Cheche, "The dishes and things are washed. I'll go over and get started making dough."

"We'll be right over," said Cheche with a smile.

"Sergio, I suppose you have never made bread," he said with a grin.

"I've seen my mother do it when I was a child. That's all I know."

"As far as anyone is concerned, you are a bakery helper. It is quiet out here where we're at, and I rarely have anyone come to the bakery. But I'd rather not take any chances, so you must work in the bakery all day."

"I am happy to do that, of course!"

"I'll take you over and show you what you can do to keep busy in the garage and bakery. Then I'm going to go see someone about a plan for you."

Salvador felt a slight chill. I just can't help but have doubts. My life is in his hands. Calm down, Sal. Trust him. There's no alternative right now.

China had little to say after Cheche departed in the truck. Salvador brought bread box trays from the truck into the bakery to be loaded with fresh loaves for delivery. Then he went into the garage side of the bakery warehouse and kept quietly busy doing nothing. Later, when sheets of loaves began to come out of the ovens, their delicious smell wafted into the garage. That was his cue to go and savor the air filled with the rich aroma of freshly baked Cuban bread. But more importantly, to help China to move them from the sheets onto wooden tables to cool. Once cooled, he put the loaves in dozen-loaf box trays for loading into the truck when Cheche returned.

She broke her long silence by asking, "How long will you be here?"

"Until Cheche can find me a job and place to live." She knows damn well the Ministry of Interior has eyes and ears everywhere. Don't I know it. I can't blame her for being afraid of someone reporting me for just popping up here out of the blue.

Secretary of Defense Robert S. McNamara and National Security Advisor McGeorge Bundy entered the Oval Office, greeted the President, and stood in front of the Resolute Desk.

"Good morning, gentlemen!" said JFK.

"We'll be brief, Mr. President, but we wanted to apprise you of a situation," said Bundy. "

"I'd like to have time for a swim before lunch, if possible," said JFK.

"Ten minutes is the most we'll need, Mr. President," said Bundy.

"Good! Let's hear it," said JFK.

Bundy spoke hurriedly, "John McCone (Director, CIA) briefed me earlier on this. I spoke with Secretaries Rusk and McNamara about it on the phone. They agreed that you should know about it. Secretary Rusk's schedule precluded him from accompanying us. The short version is that the CIA covertly put a Navy radio intercept operator into Cuba to try and glean some communications intelligence about offensive weapons coming in from the Soviet Union. The operator's cover was possibly blown relatively quickly. He was arrested and imprisoned in his attempt to get to Guantanamo Naval Station."

JFK turned to McNamara, "What is your recommendation for action, Mr. Secretary?"

"At this juncture, Dean and I both feel we should just watch this one closely," said McNamara. "CIA is not sure the Cuban government knows he's a U.S. agent."

Bundy interjected, "Nor do we know the circumstances of his arrest. John told us he's a fluent Spanish speaker of Cuban descent, so this could resolve itself without implicating the U.S."

"Did the agent have enough time to learn anything?" asked JFK.

"He reported excellent quality COMINT on the existence of mobile anti-ship surface-to-surface launchers," said Bundy, quickly adding, "Photo-reconnaissance verification has not yet been obtained."

"What's the worst outcome of his arrest?" asked JFK.

"They could aggressively interrogate him and learn that he's a covert agent. Possibly even learn what we know about offensive weapon developments there."

"The potential danger in that event is that they would surely tell the Soviets, who may plan some preemptive action," said McNamara.

JFK sat back in his chair, in deep thought, for a moment. "We'll take no action at this time. Mac, get Secretaries Rusk and McNamara, John McCone, General Taylor, and you on my calendar as a priority this afternoon before I leave for Newport. I'd like to discuss this further. Have some options for me to consider."

At the sound of the garage door being opened, Salvador went into the garage, anxious to learn more about his fate.

"Hello, Cheche! Any news for me?"

"I'll learn more later, maybe tomorrow, Sergio. That's all I can say for now."

Openly disappointed, Salvador took a deep breath, "I can wait another day."

"It might be more than one day. Perhaps many days. Be patient. This is not going to be easy to do."

"I understand, and I appreciate all you are doing for me. The loaves are all boxed and ready to load into the truck after lunch. China has gone to the house to prepare it."

The next day, Salvador and Cheche were loading boxes of loaves into the truck when they heard the sound of a vehicle pulling up to the garage.

"Quick, go to the house and wait in your bedroom!" Cheche said to Salvador.

A while later, Cheche knocked on Salvador's bedroom door, "I am coming in to tell you what I have learned."

"Come in. That wait felt like hours," said Salvador.

"My boss has decided to try and get you to the Navy air base early tomorrow morning. Sundays are best because most officials, police, and military are not working. The others are less vigilant. He also thinks it's too dangerous for us to wait until next Sunday. We can't keep you here any longer. They are looking for the attackers of that truck, us, and the escaped prisoners."

"I know a lot about the perimeter road gate to the Naval Air Station on the western side of the mouth of Guantanamo Bay if that helps your decision."

"The boss has given us different orders."

"I don't know much about other gates. What is your plan?"

"We can get you safely to a shoreline west of the Navy air base."

"How close?"

"I don't know. That is all the information that the boss gave me."

15 – Best Laid Plans…

Captain Patterson's secure phone was ringing as he returned to his office. "Patterson!"

"I was just about to hang up, Dan. Sorry, did I wake you?" asked Jefferson with a laugh.

"As if, Marv! I just got back from the cafeteria. What have you heard?"

"I've heard that the police in Guantanamo City called the Department of Interior Headquarters in Havana to verify the driver's license and car registration of one Sergio Lopez. They confirmed the driver's license but had no record of the car."

"That means he's definitely being held in Guantanamo! Only thing is, there's a problem with the car."

"That's my take on it. But that's all I have from Cuba, for now anyway."

"Damn. You have some great sources, Marv. Well, that's more than we had, but nothing we can use. Where do we go from here?"

"Well, I do have an update for you that relates to him. Our Director briefed the White House on this situation. He didn't reveal his name or service. The result was a high-level decision to tread water, for now at least. But State and Defense were also in on that decision, so they're also aware."

"That probably stems from Admiral Kurtz, who felt it was prudent to brief the Chief of Naval Operations thoroughly on this. It appears it's gone up to the Secretary of Defense."

"Then we can be confident that SecDef made an informed opinion on this. Good. Good."

"It's interesting, Marv, that NSA has not picked up a thing on this. So the Cubans or Soviets don't seem to be communicating with anyone outside of Cuba, or not in the clear, anyway."

"As I said before. We just need to let this thing play out and hope for the best."

"I hate that my man has essentially been hung out to dry."

"Not exactly. You have a tendency to underestimate those anti-Castro guys. We can assume they know all about him and his whereabouts, believe me."

"Hope springs eternal, as a wise man once said!"

Salvador and Cheche left the house just after 12 a.m. and went into the garage. They waited anxiously inside the garage side door, listening for a car to arrive.

"Cheche, I sure hope they're right about it being a sleepy Sunday," Salvador said, unable to stand the silence while anxiety was building.

"We all do, Sergio," he said, patting Salvador on the shoulder.

It was impossible for Salvador to keep from beginning to pace. He felt tension building in his gut and adrenaline beginning to have its effect. Running through the plan in his mind kept him from thinking of the many unknowns ahead.

Nearly an hour passed at an excruciatingly slow pace before the sounds of a car approaching in the quiet of the night got their attention. "This must be your car," Cheche whispered. The engine noise grew louder until it stopped in front of the garage, followed by a squeaking car door.

Cheche opened the door when he heard a soft knock.

"Good, you are ready. I am Nilda."

"This is Sergio; he's your rider," Cheche said softly.

"Hello, sir. We will leave right away. If you packed a bag, leave it behind," she said and walked to the car.

Salvador gripped Cheche's shoulder, "Thank you, sir, for

everything!'"

"Good luck, Sergio." They shook hands with gusto.

Salvador walked quickly to the car. He smiled in the scant light the slice of moon provided. Now there's a classic, a 47 Chevy 2-door. Looks like a sun-bleached light blue paint job, probably with house paint and a lot of rust. I hope the floorboard doesn't look through to the road.

She started the car as soon as he opened the noisy door. The dome light came on and gave him a good look at Nilda. She can't even be 30. She might be brave, but does she have the experience for this? As soon as he sat down and closed the door, she hit the gas.

"Where are you taking me?"

"Don't ask a lot of questions, Sergio," she said with unexpected authority. "I will take you as far as I think it's safe. If we get stopped, I will do the talking."

Damn, maybe she does have more than just guts. "I understand. Thank you for helping me." I'd sure like a few details, like exactly where I'm going, so I can visualize the map in my mind. Cheche mentioned a shoreline, so I guess I'll be walking along the beach or swimming.

"If you are trying to get to the Navy base, you must be an American. How did you get into Cuba?"

"I swam." I'm sure she won't believe that. Curious, girl too. At least she knows where I want to go.

She laughed, "I appreciate that you don't want to talk about it. I'm just glad you came here to help us. Castro and his people have caused many of us much pain and suffering."

"Mmhmm." She's right. I don't want to talk about it. I need to get her off my story. "How has this regime affected you?"

While she spoke, the dashboard lights allowed him to see that she remained alert and kept her eyes on the road and the rearview mirror. She never turned her head toward him. "My father was an accountant for a large gas station and auto service center. We had a nice house and property. My family had a comfortable and peaceful life. When they seized our property, my father spoke too openly against Castro's communism. A truck full of soldiers pulled up one evening and gave us an hour to get our things."

"Nilda, that must have been horrible!"

"Clearly! My brother and I were hysterical. When my brother lost his temper and struck one of the soldiers, they shot and killed him. My mother and father saw it all. They were never the same after that."

He saw her wipe her eyes. "I'm so sorry you and your family had to go through all that. I just can't imagine it."

"My parents became furious, which gave them an excuse to arrest us. They put my father, mother, and me in a prison cell together for about two weeks. We were taken to a cane farm where they used my father as a field worker."

"What did they do with you and your mother??"

"We washed and mended clothes and made meals with what little food they gave us. We were so hungry all the time."

He could hear the anger in her voice. "It's a cruel regime that only claims to be for the good of all the people."

"A lie is what that is. My father was simply worked to death. Meningitis spread through the workers. The bosses thought they were revolting and not working as hard as they could and ignored their illnesses. My father died in the field." She wiped her eyes with trembling fingers and said emotionally, "Mom got sick with something that took her life quickly. She died in her sleep; it was awful."

Salvador's gut was churning. "I know why you are doing this now. How did you get free?"

"The wife of the cane farm manager took me as her inside housekeeper when she caught two soldiers trying to rape me while I was hanging clothes on a line." She got quiet.

He waited for her eyes to dry before asking, "How did you get free?"

"While eating lunch in my room in their cellar, she came down and told me she had something important to tell me. Her husband had arranged to free me. So she asked me if I had someone she could take me to."

"That must have shocked you!"

"I was suspicious. I didn't tell her anyone's name or where I was going. I just asked her to take me to a place that was about a twenty-minute walk from where my aunt and uncle lived. I live with them now."

"What a story. I hope you and so many of the Cuban people who have suffered will be happy one day soon. Are your relatives as anti-Castro as you? I'm sorry, you don't have to answer."

She didn't answer that and said nothing more for several minutes.

"You would think, after all I have told you, that I would be a suicidal recluse, but I chose to live. *'Patria o Muerte,'* my country or my life, is a terrible choice this regime offers us." She paused with a sniffle.

His mind soaked up the deep sentiments she revealed. I can't help but feel her pain. He was about to speak when she continued.

"Sergio, without liberty, we might as well be dead!"

He could hear intense emotions in her voice. "Well said, Nilda." Better words escaped him as his gut clenched.

Bumpy unimproved roads woke Salvador from a short nap. He tilted his wrist to catch the light from the dash instruments so he could see his watch. 13 minutes! That was a short nap. We're already in the boonies. I'll try asking again. "Cheche mentioned that you're taking me to a shoreline. How far from the air station will it be?"

She hesitated. "I think about five miles, maybe less."

He felt a fleeting tightness in his gut. "Oh! That's farther than I expected."

"I told you I would get you as close as I could safely! For both of us."

"What's the shoreline like?"

"I'm not sure about the whole walk you will have. I have only seen parts a few times. My father took the family for rides along the shoreline road before Castro took over. We used to park and go down to the beach for picnics. It was rocky, but some places had a nice sandy beach."

"Did you notice how much tidal change there was?"

"I remember walking down to a place that had a nice beach area. One time we went there, the waves were hitting the rocks."

"What about beach patrols?"

"There's a road that runs along the shore for a long way, but I doubt the beach is closer than 100 feet and only in places. I know they patrol the road regularly most of the day and night, but not by foot. They patrol in pairs in small open vehicles. But they park and sleep in the early hours of the morning, especially Sunday."

"I hope they are tired tonight. What do you know about the fence at the shoreline at the air station?"

"They told me to tell you there are guard stations along that fence."

"Good. I hope they'll be able to see me well enough to keep from mistaking me as an armed intruder."

"Since it is a clear night, with some moonlight, you should be able to make your way along the shoreline and be seen plainly by the Marine guards. If there's an outer fence, don't try to get past it. The Marines have probably mined that part."

"There's no easy part of this trip, Nilda. How much farther is it?"

"I'm driving slow to keep the engine noise down. Maybe twenty more minutes."

Oh my God, the longest twenty minutes of my life. And then it's just the beginning of a long walk, which doesn't sound like an easy one.

Salvador couldn't help but be on edge, searching ahead for cars, jeeps, trucks, walkers, and whatever might be out of order. Minutes crept by.

"See that turn to the left way up there?" she asked.

"Umm, yes."

"That is as close to the water as I can get you, so that is where you get out."

A shiver ran through his gut. He felt his ears get hot, and his heart begin to pound. Oh shit, here we go.

"I'm going to stop while turning around. As soon as I stop, get out and hurry to the shore."

"Thank you for doing this. Good luck, Nilda."

"Good luck to you!"

Fifty yards from the turn, headlights came around the corner and were heading toward them.

"Can you see what it is?" she asked.

"No, the headlights are all I can see."

It was mere seconds before they realized the headlights were coming straight at them. She slowed to a creep and steered to the far right side of the road, two tires on a rough shoulder.

"It's a jeep, and they're not going to let you pass."

She stopped the car, rolled down her window, and waited. The jeep stopped several feet directly in front of them.

"Stay calm, Sergio. I'll try and talk us through this."

The soldier driving stood up and pointed a rifle at the car, while the other soldier kept his handgun pointed at the car as he got out of the jeep and approached.

"Show me your driver's license and car registration!" the soldier ordered in a harsh tone with a Colt-45 pointed at her head.

"Of course, Corporal," she said calmly.

Salvador opened the glove compartment and got out the registration while she got her license out of her purse.

"What's your name?" the Corporal asked her.

"Nilda Garcia."

Fighting off nervousness and anxiety, Salvador knew he'd be next. Should I make up a new name? No, I can't get caught lying to the police if that's what it comes down to. This guy probably won't know I'm a wanted man.

After the Corporal examined her papers with a flashlight, he turned the flashlight to Salvador. "You! What's your name?"

"Sergio Lopez."

"I want to see your driver's license."

"I don't drive. I have nothing else to show you."

The Corporal paused. "Is Nilda your wife?"

"No, not yet." He knew Nilda would pick up on that storyline.

Turning the flashlight back to Nilda, the Corporal asked, "This is Alberto Garcia's car. Who is he?"

"My father. I live with my parents."

"You're far from Caimanera. What are you two doing out here this time of night?"

"Living with our parents gives us no privacy. We come out here to be alone by the sea. The moon is so beautiful reflecting on the water."

Shaking his head, the Corporal signaled to the driver, then said gruffly, "I don't believe you. Get out of the car, both of you."

16 - Havana Luxury

S alvador and Nilda were handcuffed and taken to the police headquarters in Caimanera. They shared a disgusting prison cell, stripped to their undergarments, without food or water until the next morning, Monday, September 10.

Huddled together, they watched as a guard came to their cell, opened the door, threw their clothes in, and left without a word.

"I didn't have anything hidden in my clothes, did you?" she whispered.

"No."

"They have nothing then. They'll just put us to work somewhere for a while."

"There's one problem, Nilda," he whispered close to her ear. "A few days before you picked me up, I escaped from the police prison in Guantanamo. If they check the name I gave when they stopped us, we'll both be in trouble."

She turned away, began to tremble, and suffered a few dry heaves.

During the next two days, Salvador and Nilda were questioned individually and extensively several times. In the afternoon of the second day, the prison history and escape of Sergio Lopez were uncovered. Salvador and Nilda were in deeper trouble than they knew.

During the evening hours of Wednesday, September 12, without explanation, Salvador and Nilda were transferred to the Villa Marista secret police detention center in Havana. They occupied cells in opposite corners of, for lack of a better term, a dungeon with no windows. It was poorly lit, grossly smelling, cramped for maximum prisoner capacity, and severely austere. There was no mattress, no pillow, and no blanket. But he did have a wooden bucket, which was hideously stained, stinking, and sickening to even look at even in dim light. I guess there's a standard for prison cell furnishings, he thought.

Exhausted, he tried to find a comfortable position to get to sleep. It seemed impossible. The cement floor was rock hard, cold, felt damp, and moldy in the corners. His mind refused to shut down and meandered randomly. Where the hell am I? As long as it took for them to get me here, it's got to be Havana. I'm in for some serious interrogation. Oh, Nilda, you wouldn't be here suffering all this if not for me. That's something I'll have to live with for the rest of my life. God knows how long that will be. If I am in Havana, I can expect to be tortured for every last tidbit of information I have. On the other hand, if that's where I'm at, the odds may be better for DC to find out that I'm here. For all the good that will do. They'll probably have to claim no knowledge of me. Nobody's going to get my sorry ass out of this place. Why did I volunteer? Everyone, including me, thought all the Is were dotted and the Ts were crossed. It will be impossible to get out of this mess. Salvador's gut was churning. Oh, God, forgive me for what I've done to Nilda and the sadness I'll cause Angela and Mom and Dad. Finally, shock and exhaustion forced him to drift into a light sleep.

During the night, Salvador repeatedly drifted in and out of a stupor-like sleep. He woke to a strange sound, his mind hazy. Two armed men in military fatigues unlocked his cell door and entered.

"Get up!" ordered a man wearing corporal stripes.

"Yes, sir!"

"Don't speak!"

The guards lost patience with his slow, fumbling attempt to stand due to being stiff and sore from sleeping on the hard floor and sleeplessness. They pulled him up gruffly, handcuffed him with his hands behind him, and took him by the arms to an interrogation room.

Don't these guys shower? Their body odor is almost as bad as my bucket.

Interrogation Room 2 was about 8'x10' with cement walls and floor. It had no windows. The guards plunked him onto a wooden chair in the center, facing the back wall, with his arms draped behind the chair's back. They stood at motionless parade rest on each side of the door facing him.

Trying to find calm was impossible for Salvador. I know some cruel sarcastic bastard will come in here and beat the hell out of me, and I'm helpless. Stick to the story you gave them at the Guantanamo jail.

The sound of the door opening and slamming shut sent a bolt of ice through his gut. A short man wearing lieutenant bars walked in briskly and stood in front of him with his arms crossed, staring eerily, silently, for hours, or so it seemed. The silence was deafening. Salvador could hear his heart pounding in his ears and could feel it in his chest.

"What is your name, criminal?" the Lieutenant suddenly yelled.

They took my fingerprints when they arrested me in Guantanamo and again last night. He already knows or will soon. "Sergio Lopez, sir."

"Where do you live?"

"I was in the process of moving when I was arrested by the Soviets. They transferred me to the Guantanamo police." No sign of surprise. He knows.

The Lieutenant questioned Salvador for over an hour. He asked about the circumstances of the original arrest by the Soviets and Salvador's life history. He got the same information as the Guantanamo police.

Stepping back and staring again for moments, the Lieutenant said gruffly, "I think you are a big liar. There's something wrong in some or all of that." He abruptly kicked the chair seat hard between Salvador's legs. The back of Salvador's head hit the cement floor when the chair toppled backward. He cried out from the pain in his arms that took his full weight when he fell backward onto them. The guards were waved off when they began to move toward Salvador to get him back onto a righted chair.

It took a minute for the Lieutenant to see that Salvador was coming to his senses. He stood straddled over Salvador, leaned down, pointed a pistol at the side of his head, and asked with an evil-sounding whisper, " How do you know the woman you were arrested with?"

She's going to look out for her own ass, and I better do the same. "I never saw her before in my life. The people who captured me from the work site in Guantanamo wanted to move me, and she got the job."

"Where were they taking you?"

"I don't know, sir. She wouldn't say."

"Liar!" shouted the Lieutenant and kicked Salvador in the ribs.

Stunned momentarily by the pain, the cobwebs cleared slowly. "I'm not lying, sir."

The guards came over and righted him in the chair when the Lieutenant nodded to them.

"Where did they take you after they captured you?"

"I don't know, sir, and they wouldn't tell me," he said, staring into the muzzle of the Lieutenant's Makarov pistol.

"How long was the drive?"

He's not going to put a round into my head. He's far from done questioning. "Maybe 20 minutes, sir. I'm not sure. It was very confusing."

"Did you know any of them before that?"

"No, sir."

"What was the place like where they took you?"

Oh, shit, I hate giving up much, but it better sound good, or I'll be in for more pain. "It was just a garage for a truck. They kept me there until that woman came and took me away."

"Did you hear any names?"

"Nobody used names. Not even that woman driver."

"Why did they capture you?"

"I do not know. It was unexpected and scary. They kept my handcuffs on until they put me in that car with the woman."

"She didn't say anything about where you were being taken? Or why?"

"Nothing, sir! I asked, but all she said was I would find out."

"Who are you?"

"Sergio Lopez, sir."

"That is what is on the driver's license that was given to our Guantanamo office. But we know that is a lie! Don't be a fool. Tell me who you really are!"

Salvador hid his surprise. *Damn, he knows all there is to know. I hope he doesn't see holes in my stories. If I tell him who I am, I'm a dead man for sure. Hanging onto being Sergio delays death and keeps them wondering.* "Sir, I am Sergio Lopez. That is not a lie. This all started with a mistaken arrest by the Soviets. Simple as that!"

Leaning down close to Salvador's ear, the Lieutenant forcefully whispered, "Why do you keep telling lies. I will hear the truth from your mouth soon! Or you will stand before a firing squad. That is your choice!"

"You heard the truth, sir!"

"Not yet!" the Lieutenant yelled loudly into Salvador's ear. "But I will soon!"

Salvador saw the punch coming and spread his feet for stability. He couldn't move his head enough to have it glance. The powerful impact on his left cheek would have sent him to the floor again were it not for his leg strength. The pain was awful. Bright twinkling stars flashed and sparkled, whether his eyes were open or closed. The hollow-sounding voice of the Lieutenant echoed in his ears.

"Corporal, take him to Room 99 and strap him to the table."

Captain Patterson was just finishing his Sunday brunch at home when the phone rang.

"Good morning, this is Dan."

"Mornin' Dan, it's Marv. The good part remains to be seen. I have location news on your man. Call me when you get to work."

As soon as Captain Patterson arrived at his office, he dialed his secure phone. "OK, Marv, what have you found out?"

"I called your office. They told me you went home last night. Doesn't a good meal or two and a decent shower feel good??

"Yes, but let's get to the meat, Marv."

Jefferson chuckled, "In a nutshell, the Op Mongoose guys in Miami

109

said they have info that says Sergio Lopez is in the Department of Interior jail in Havana. I think it's solid info."

"How in the world did he wind up there?"

"That's all we know. Someone on the jail staff reports all new prisoners to their contact. He was imprisoned there three days ago. That is all we know."

"What possible courses of action do we have?"

"My boss says we just wait for further developments."

"That's hard to swallow, Marv. If I take that kind of news to Admiral Kurtz again, he's not going to be pleasant about it. Are you sure that's CIA's best plan of action?"

"I know, Dan. It's not easy for me either. But my boss said he'd be briefing the Director about this on Monday morning. Hold off with your boss until we get a response from McCone."

"Marv, I just can't hold off. He'll have my head. But I'll let him know when your boss is briefing the Director."

"Fair enough, my friend. We'll talk again for sure on Monday morning after my boss get's back from the briefing."

17 – Horse Trade

Wednesday afternoon, September 19, 1962, in Washington, DC, was pleasant with temperatures in the 70s, although humid and cloudy with rain seemingly imminent. Life, like the weather overall, was good. Even though the public was aware that the cold war was escalating slowly, it seemed only like political posturing. However, a restricted number of people in the intelligence community and the White House knew the details of what the Soviets were up to in Cuba, which was potentially ominous. The mainstream press was aware of a Soviet buildup in Cuba. It was, of course, suspicious, but they had no appreciation for the extent of the Soviet plan for Cuba. For the intelligence community, the Soviet plan was clear, but incontrovertible evidentiary pieces of the threat puzzle were yet to be laid down. Most frustrated with those missing pieces was President Kennedy. Every day, the Presidential Daily Briefing contained more intelligence on the Soviet Union's rapidly growing military operations in Cuba. There was a high volume of cargo ship deliveries, much of it undisclosed in shipping documents and crated to hide the contents from all forms of reconnaissance. Overflights and satellites detected accelerated military construction at sites throughout the island with familiar and alarming characteristics. However, the veritable smoking gun remained an inch from discovery. Nearly a week had passed since Salvador was imprisoned in Havana. This afternoon, President Kennedy will hear his name for the first time.

Greetings were exchanged with the President by Secretary of State Dean Rusk, Director of Central Intelligence John McCone, Attorney General Robert Kennedy, Special Counsel Theodore Sorensen, and Special Assistant to the President for National Security Affairs, McGeorge 'Mac' Bundy as they filed into the Oval Office.

JFK motioned for them to take seats on the opposing couches in the middle of the room as he left his desk to get comfortable in a rocking chair facing them.

"Mr. Secretary, you were on my calendar, but I see you brought a few friends," JFK said with a curious tone.

"Yes, Mr. President. There's been a development you need to know about," said Rusk, nodding at McCone.

"I briefed you previously about a covert military agent in Cuba, Mr. President," said McCone, taking a deep breath.

"Yes, John, I recall," said JFK. "A Navy intercept operator."

"Yes, sir. It's Communications Technician Salvador Conte," said McCone. "The short version of the situation I'm briefing this afternoon is that we have a report from a Cuban informant that Conte and an accomplice, a woman, were arrested and are being held in the Cuban Department of Interior jail in Havana."

"Do we know the circumstances that led to the arrest?" asked Sorensen.

"And who's the woman?" asked Robert Kenndy.

"I wish I had answers to both of those questions, gentlemen," McCone said with a shrug. "All we know right now is that Conte departed by car on August 27 on a two-day drive, alone, headed for the Naval Air Station at Guantanamo. What happened between the 27th and the 12th and where or how the woman comes into the picture is unknown to the Agency."

Bundy sat forward, "My concern, John, is that he'll be interrogated and could reveal intelligence that we don't want the Soviets to know just yet. What does he know? What is the potential damage?"

McCone nodded, "First, I was told he was selected for this mission because he has not been involved in anything really sensitive so far in his career. Second, his briefings at the CIA and NSA did not involve highly sensitive methods and sources and were limited strictly to what he absolutely needed to know for the mission. But I'm concerned about what he learned down there and what he could reveal about our informants he has contacted. Thus, we're treating this as a blown cover incident for those and other reasons, which you'll hear about."

"Will your informant that reported his jailing know if Conte talks?" asked Bundy.

"That's highly improbable. However, that jail does not shy from aggressive interrogation or torture. It may be just a matter of time before they break him. My clandestine ops officer said that he's tough and disciplined."

"Yes, but every man has a limit," said JFK, frowning. "I don't see what we can do about this. Any thoughts?"

"Oh, there's more to this, Mr. President," said Bundy, turning to Rusk and sitting back.

Rusk nodded to Bundy and looked at JFK, "I met with Ambassador Dobrynin this morning. He brought a prisoner trade proposal from President Fidel Castro. They want to trade Cuban Army Colonel Cordaro Escalante and a million dollars for CIA agent Sergio Lopez. Premier Kruschev added another million and Arseny Voronin to the trade, as a price, if you will, for performing intermediary functions in the trade negotiations."

McCone interjected, "By the way, Sergio Lopez is the cover name for the Navy man in question, Petty Officer Conte. The fact that they didn't identify him as a Navy agent tells me they only have strong suspicions about who he is and are assuming that he's CIA. But," McCone continued with emphasis, "we absolutely don't know."

Rusk added, "I have to advise that by pursuing this trade, we confirm to the Cubans and Soviets that he's a valuable asset."

"That's certainly the case," said McCone. "The other side of the coin is that dismissing Conte as a worthwhile trade would be putting our signature on Conte's death warrant."

"This horse trade is quite an interesting gambit but ridiculously expensive," said Robert Kennedy. "They are sure enough that he might be a viable trade, or they'd just kill him as an intolerable rebel Cuban. The money is just a negotiating point, I'm sure."

Rusk nodded, "I think Dobrynin has been instructed to drag these trade negotiations out to allow the KGB to have their own interrogators continue working on Conte. He seems to be in no hurry. But more importantly, it serves to distract us while the Soviets get more time for the offensive weapons to become operational. At this point in time, the Cubans will do whatever the Soviets tell them to do."

"So, about this Colonel, how valuable is he to them?" asked JFK.

"Oh, very!" said Robert Kennedy. "The Cubans are serious about him. For background, Colonel Escalante was part of the Cuban Embassy's Attaché staff here in DC. The FBI learned that he was getting disenchanted with Castro's regime, so they were talking with him, actually cultivating him to be a double agent or seek asylum. He got cold feet, sensing he was being watched by his superiors and tried to capture our agent to save face. Fortunately, they had serious doubts about Escalante and had backup for that last meeting. The FBI arrested him in the act. He was subsequently convicted of kidnapping, attempted murder, and espionage. He's currently being held in federal prison. The Cubans have sent several letters via Dobrynin to get him released and returned."

McCone added, "We have learned that he was one of Fidel's fair-haired boys. He gave them advance information on the Bay of Pigs operation and was being groomed for promotion to general."

"Aside from taking advantage of some leverage, why does Dobrynin want this Russian?" asked JFK

"Another complicated story," said Rusk.

"That it is," said Robert Kennedy. "Director Hoover briefed me that Voronin was a KGB agent assigned to the Soviet Consulate in San Franciso. He approached a State Department secretary in our Passport Agency there. She was smart enough to report Voronin to her supervisor right away. The FBI orchestrated her interactions with him. The bottom line is that he's in a safe house in Virginia and has requested asylum. I'm sure the Soviets want him back to, uh," he chuckled, "fill a position in a gulag or to occupy an unmarked burial plot in a forest somewhere."

JFK thought deeply while he digested all he had heard. "Wouldn't there be a problem with returning an asylum applicant, Bobby?"

"There's precedent for that, of course," said Robert Kennedy. "But, morally, we would have to formally reject the application beforehand. If we trade him after officially approving Voronin's plea? Oh, that would be a horse of a different color. Our national reputation, especially for asylum seekers, would be damaged. I'll have to check on the status of his request. Dean, be sure no such approval action is pursued in State until we get this sorted out."

JFK looked at his watch, stopped rocking, and slapped both palms on the arms of the rocker. "It's time for us to move into the Cabinet Room and join the others for today's Cuba briefing. I'll sleep on this. We'll talk more about it tomorrow. Let's not bring any of this up in the Cabinet Room. Keep it among those of us here for now. We'll bring others in on it as needed later."

Salvador leaned back against the wall after finishing what he guessed was breakfast, which consisted of a scant handful of crunchy uncooked rice swimming in a small bowl of water. His mind was troubled by seeing that Nilda was still not in her cell. She was absent when he returned from the awful interrogation he got yesterday. She either talked herself out of jail or… A gut-wrenching chill went through his body. I don't even want to think of that. He said a mental prayer for her safety.

The lack of windows, the seemingly random arrival of food and water, or other clues to time passage caused him to lose track of days and dates. Eyes closed, his mind created mental vignettes of Angela. Her soft voice echoed tauntingly in his head. He felt her silken hair teasing his face and neck. Images of his mother and father were interspersed with myriad flashbacks of good times in his life. Mental images and memories gave him the only luxuries he had. Sleep deprivation, caused by the discomforts of the bare cement floor and the brutality of the interrogations, was simultaneously causing brief drifts into sleep, euphoria, anxiety, and increasing difficulty hanging onto sanity. So far, his strong self-discipline was winning.

The clatter of the jail cell door being unlocked and the squeal of old dry hinges jolted him back to full consciousness. Oh, shit! Time for another friendly conversation with that ruthless bastard. I've got to stick to my story, or they'll just kill me.

Guards took him cuffed and in leg shackles into Interrogation Room 2, one he'd seen before, but the desk was gone, and only a chair remained. They sat him down roughly onto the chair, his cuffed arms behind the back of it. The guards then stood back by the door.

This is a nice change from the torture room. I'm still not looking forward to this.

A Soviet officer entered the room and stood in front of him, staring and smiling.

Salvador was stunned. Oh, this is crazy; it's that damn KGB Lieutenant from the missile base.

"Sergio Lopez, we meet again," Travkin said with a sinister tone and strong Russian accent. "The colonel gave me your car to drive back to Havana. It is a nice one. My superior is driving it now. But why did you remove all the car identifications?"

"I didn't do that, Lieutenant. It's how it was when I bought it."

"I have read all the reports of your questioning. I don't believe any of it. I want to know who you are and what you are doing in Cuba?"

"Just a Cuban patriot who returned to his homeland."

After another hour of questioning, Travkin said, "I do not believe much of what you have told me or the others. I think you are very good at telling lies and tolerating much pain, Lopez. Time will tell whether you live or die. If it were my decision, a firing squad would be too good for you. But I have my orders. Guards, take him back to his cell."

He has his orders. I can only wonder what the hell that means. I hope it's going to be good. Come on, DC, get my ass out of this shit hole.

In the following days, there was no further torture or interrogation. Meals, such as they were, increased to three times daily with a little more rice in the water. Although a welcome change, it was both disconcerting and hopeful.

18 – Complex Choreography

Secretary of State Dean Russ haggled with Ambassador Dobrynin every day for over a week regarding the trade proposal. Every option Rusk offered was summarily rejected. The only wiggle room there seemed to be was with the money. It had been exhausting. Rusk was under pressure from the White House to complete the trade promptly. Intelligence was strong that the situation was rapidly coming to a head. If the trade wasn't completed before the Soviets were confronted with hard evidence of their offensive weapons in Cuba, it would be impossible to do the deal.

Information that Salvador reported regarding the location and numbers of Soviet portable anti-ship missile systems was influential in focusing reconnaissance assets to find them. Other human intelligence from Cuba led to the discovery of several apparent strategic missile installations being built rapidly throughout the island. The President was informed that the strategic systems could become operational by November or sooner. The race was on.

Rusk finally got the terms, timing, and procedures for the trade finalized. Cuba would get Colonel Escalante and a half-million dollars. The Soviet Union would get Arseny Voronin and a half-million dollars. The trade would be accomplished in a complex choreography of actions in the U.S. and Cuba on Monday, October 1, 1962.

Salvador awoke, stood up, and stretched. His back and joints ached from sleeping in his clothes on the concrete floor of the cell. While everyone was still sleeping, including the guard in the middle of the room, he began pacing quietly around his cell. My gut is growling so loud it could wake people up. Oh, my God, I thought something good was going to happen, but it's not. This isn't good. Stop it, Sal. You can't let them get to you. I'll think about Angela, mom, and dad.

An hour of pacing stopped when he heard the door to the cell block being opened, giving him hope it was food. Empty-handed guards came to his cell, handcuffed him, took him to Interrogation Room #2, and took off the cuffs.

"Do not talk. Take off all your clothes and underwear. Put them in the bag by the chair. Put on the clothes you see on the chair." An unmarked olive drab jumpsuit sat in a pile on the chair seat.

Salvador held back a smile. Oh, gladly. Getting out of these wretched clothes is a pleasure. No underwear. Good grief, these are way too big.

The guards put his cuffs back on and led him up steps and along halls, then out into the already hot, painfully bright morning sun.

Fresh air! Damn, I forgot how wonderful that smells and feels. What the hell is going on? "Where am I going?"

"Quiet! Do not speak!"

Shortly, a jeep pulled up near the fence in front of the building. The guards took him through the gate. "Get in the back. If you try to jump out, you'll be shot."

After a wild 20-minute jeep ride, Salvador saw they were entering Jose Marti airport. The jeep passed through two checkpoints and stopped in front of a hangar.

Sweating profusely in the heat, Salvador's mind rambled. Looks like I'm getting a free flight to Russia. The weather will be a lot cooler in Siberia. The sun's angle tells me it's about 1400. Thank you, mother nature, for the shade in front of this hangar. This is one damn busy airport. He noted many Soviet fighters parked on nearby aprons with uniformed men scurrying about them and nearby hangars. A commercial airliner landed, taxied to a terminal, and deplaned passengers. It was too far away to read the writing on its fuselage, but he could tell it wasn't Soviet or Cuban. The smell of kerosene teased his nostrils. A jet engine began wailing on a test stand somewhere, blocking out all other sounds for a few minutes.

Salvador started to ask, "What..."

"Shut up! Don't talk!" a guard said angrily.

It was a good half-hour before Salvador watched the speck of a distant plane start its approach to the runway.

Oh, my God. I hope I'm not hallucinating, thought Salvador when he realized it was a C-130 cargo plane on a short final, with a beautiful U.S. flag emblazoned on its tail. His eyes stayed glued on it while it landed and taxied in front of the hangar, stopping only 20 yards away.

Heart pounding, his breathing more rapid, Salvador watched and waited. Nothing was happening.

After many agonizing minutes, two armed Cuban soldiers, a man in civilian clothes, and a Cuban Army officer came out of a hangar door and walked midway to the aircraft. The C-130's rear ramp lowered with a soft thud. A man in a 3-piece suit and six Marines armed with AR-15 rifles walked down the ramp. The Marines took up positions around the aircraft. The U.S. civilian approached the Cuban civilian and had a short conversation. One of the Cuban soldiers accompanied the U.S. representative to the jeep, where Salvador waited, shaking with a mix of shock and anticipation.

"Mr. Lopez, I'm with the U.S. State Department. I am here to return you to the United States."

Tears began streaming from Salvador's eyes. "Sir, I've never wanted anything more in my life."

The U.S. representative turned to the Cuban representative, "Please allow Mr. Lopez to accompany me to the exchange point."

Salvador's cuffs were removed, and he was free to exit the jeep.

"Please walk with me on my left, Mr. Lopez. We will stop midway. Be calm."

"With pleasure, sir."

When the U.S. representative arrived at the midpoint, with several feet of separation from the Cubans, he gave the aircraft a thumbs-up sign. Another civilian, carrying an aluminum attaché case, escorted Colonel Escalante, in his dress uniform, to the Cubans. The attaché case changed hands to the Cuban civilian.

"Welcome back to Cuba, Colonel," the Cuban civilian said, shaking Escalante's hand vigorously.

"I am very happy to be back," said the Colonel, wiping tears from his eyes.

The U.S. civilian representatives exchanged nods and escorted their prize, CT1 Salvador Conte, to the C-130.

Stepping onto the aircraft's cargo ramp, the U.S. State Department representative said, "Mr. Lopez, take your seat quickly. We'll be departing immediately."

I can't believe my feet are off Cuban soil. First day of October! What a day.

The Marines quickly left their perimeter posts around the aircraft and hustled up the ramp. The sounds of the ramp closing and engines starting were heard before Salvador could get to his seat.

"What happens next, sir? Where are we going?" asked Salvador as he secured his seatbelt.

The representative spoke loudly over the din of engine noise as the aircraft quickly began taxiing. "It will be a short trip to the Naval Air Station at Key West. A medical team is waiting there to examine you. After you get cleaned up and into some clean clothes, a debriefing team will speak with you. I was told that they have obtained your dress uniform. That's as much as I know."

Salvador began tearing profusely. That means Angela gave them my uniform, so she knows I'm OK and coming home. She must be puzzled about the uniform. I left the house in uniform with a seabag. What did they tell her? What can I tell her?

As per the negotiated agreement, upon receiving a phone notification that confirmed the safe landing of the C-130 aircraft at Key West, a Secret Service limousine departed the State Department carrying Arseny Voronin. It stopped at the Soviet Embassy, where Soviet Ambassador Dobrynin received a small aluminum suitcase from a State Department civilian, along with Voronin.

19 – Homecoming

Captain Patterson and Agent Jefferson were notified that the specific C-130 they were waiting for was in contact with approach control. They went outside the hangar that had been commandeered on short notice by the CIA. A Navy medical team waited in a Navy medically configured mobile home that was parked inside the hangar. It was there to make an initial assessment of Salvador's overall health, to get him shaved, showered, a haircut, and into his whites.

"We should formally thank the State Department for getting him out of there, Dan," said Jefferson.

"Admiral Kurtz already asked me to draft a letter and has talked with Secretary Rusk."

"We're writing one also. It's smart to butter them up, even though they're bureaucratic, full of red tape, and get in my way more than I like," Jefferson said with a chuckle. "I should have known better than to wear a suit to Key West in October. I'm jealous of your short-sleeve whites, Dan."

Patterson laughed, "Even summer whites are hot in 86 degrees and 74 percent humidity. My armpits are wet. Damn, I'm happy how this turned out."

"Dan, I think that's our plane," said Jefferson when he spotted an aircraft approaching from seaward on a right-base leg for a runway 7 final approach. "It's definitely headed for NAS, not International

Airport."

"This is more excitement than I can stand, Marv."

"Yeah, it is. Getting our people back out of imminent danger is always emotional."

They watched the C-130 land, pull off onto a taxiway, and follow a Navy ground crew escort truck to the hangar.

Nearly an hour later, a Navy doctor, nurse, and two Hospital Corpsmen exited the medical mobile home. The doctor walked to Patterson and Jefferson, waiting nearby. "He's got a lot of bruises and cuts in several places; the most recent of those is about a week old. One rib has a hairline fracture that's healing just fine. According to his last Navy physical, he's lost about 30 pounds. We'll have the blood analysis results sometime tomorrow morning. Otherwise, he appears to be in good health. He's all yours."

Salvador put down a cup of orange juice, swallowed the last of a pack of cookies, and stood up, "Oh, thank you for the rescue. I was at my wit's end, Captain, Mr. Jefferson," Salvador said with a wide grin when the two of them came through the mobile home door.

"Welcome home, Conte; good to see you!" Jefferson said with a hearty handshake.

"Welcome back to the world, Conte," said Patterson, shaking Salvador's hand energetically, noting the remnants of a couple black eyes. "You lost a little weight, well, a lot of weight. Looks like you've been in a bar fight, too."

"Yes, sir. I didn't win the fight, but here I am, so I won the war. Sorry for the baggy fit on this uniform. These are my whites, alright, but I haven't been getting much to eat for quite a while. How did Angela and my parents take the news?"

Patterson slapped Salvador's shoulder, "They're very happy that you're back home. We couldn't tell them much, as you can understand. We said that you've returned from a grueling deployment and declined to give more details. I think just your being back is enough for them."

"That's good that you told them that, sir. I won't have to do a lot of tap dancing about it all."

"Yes, Conte, don't even try to explain anything."

Jefferson added, "And you can't mention my organization to anyone."

"Yes, sir, of course."

Patterson gave Salvador a quick head-to-toe and smiled, "As for your uniform, Conte, I'm sure you'll grow back into it in no time at all."

"So, when can I go home?"

"Have a seat, Conte," said Patterson. "We have an initial debriefing to perform. Then you will be flown to Bethesda Naval Hospital for a more thorough physical, X-rays, labs, the works. You've been through a lot. Some of your injuries may not be apparent. We can't take a chance."

"Our security team will also be interviewing you in-depth," Jefferson said. "There's a lot we need to know about everything that happened in Cuba."

"But I feel great now, sir, hungry as hell and thirsty, but I'm fine! Ask me what you need to know, and let me go home."

Patterson nodded, "I can appreciate how anxious you are to get home after all that's happened. It wasn't easy to arrange, but Miss Mirabol is on her way to Bethesda and will stay with you while you're there. You'll have a private room, similar to a hotel room. But you're not just a sailor coming home from an overseas tour. Meanwhile, intelligence information must be captured while still fresh in your mind, and damage assessments must be done. So, you'll be busy during the day."

Salvador's silence and blank, teary stare at the floor gave Patterson and Jefferson pause.

"OK, Conte, let me get started with some questions," Jefferson said as he looked at his watch. "There's a Navy VIP jet outside that's going to fly us to DC. But in the meantime, the first thing I want to know is, well, to be direct about it, were you tortured for information?"

"Oh, by anyone's idea of what torture is, hell yes, sir. But it all stopped about a week ago, I guess. I lost track of days. I don't even know what day it is."

"It's Monday afternoon, October 1."

"That's so hard to believe," Salvador said, shaking his head.

"Did they drug you?"

"I don't think so. Maybe. I was unconscious at least once. But I doubt it was from drugs. I don't know."

"Do you remember what you told them about what you were doing there?"

"Yeah! I stayed with the cover story I cooked up until a Russkie got involved. He threatened to pull my fingernails out with pliers unless I told the truth. I realized I had to give them some convincing information to keep him from doing that, so I told them I was a CIA agent collecting information on the location of Soviet bases." He held up both hands, "That worked. I gave them a bunch of bullshit about knowing about Soviet construction sites and the location of a couple airports where there was a lot of Soviet activity. I said I hadn't been there long enough to find a way to report my findings back to CIA. But not a damn thing about missiles..." He stopped as emotion swarmed in. He broke down.

"Relax, Conte, that's all for now," said Patterson. "You'll get a good dinner and some sleep on the plane."

"Sir, you have no idea how good..." he paused, choked up. "And comfortable sleeping is something I've been without for a long time. Do you know what happened to the girl that was arrested with me?"

Jefferson shook his head, "Sorry, Conte, we don't. But I'd like to talk more about that and more in Bethesda. Let's get aboard that jet."

The Navy VIP jet landed at Washington-National Airport in Washington, DC, and taxied to a hangar. Two limousines were waiting for them. One took Jefferson back to CIA Headquarters at Langley, Virginia; the other delivered Captain Patterson and Salvador to Bethesda Naval Hospital.

Even though expedited, admission procedures and forms seemed laborious. Patterson complied with hospital policy that required Salvador to be wheel-chaired to his room and did the honors of pushing him. A nurse met them at the elevator and led them to Salvador's room.

"This is it, Conte. I'm going to be back tomorrow after lunch. In the meantime, Jefferson and I are going to leave you to the sawbones and nurses."

"Is Angela here yet?" asked Salvador anxiously.

Patterson looked at his watch, "She'll be landing at National in about an hour. I have arranged a car to pick her up, so as soon as she gets her luggage, she'll be brought straight here and will be with you 24/7 until you're discharged."

With a broad smile, Salvador said, "I can't wait. Thank you, Captain, for everything."

"Your country thanks you, Conte!" Turning to the nurse, Patterson said, "Take good care of him. I'll get out of your hair. Do you have the approved visitors list at the nurse's station?"

"Yes, Captain, we do, and we know you're the only one authorized to change it. We'll make sure he gets a good meal and a good night's rest."

Now in a hospital gown that he despised, Salvador sat at the small round table in the corner of the room, devouring the final morsel of bacon-wrapped filet mignon. Stuffed from roast beef, mashed potatoes, and gravy aboard the plane and then the filet dinner and chocolate cake for dessert were not doing so well in his stomach. It all shocked his digestive system after such a long period of starvation. He had overdone it and was feeling queasy. He got into bed and sipped ginger ale. Not long after he pulled the sheet and blanket up and got comfortable, the now familiar knock of the nurse on his door grabbed his attention.

"Are you decent?" she called in from a cracked door.

The possibility that Angela had arrived peaked his anxiety. "Affirmative!" he blurted.

"Sal!" was the only word Angela could get out of her mouth as she rushed through the door to him, bursting into tears.

He leaped out of bed and took her into his arms. They stood hugging and kissing while the nurse brought in her two suitcases, put a "do not disturb" sign on the outside door handle, and quietly departed.

When their emotions calmed, she said with a broad smile, "That's a revealing hospital gown; your butt is hanging out." They laughed. Then the shock of the evidence of weight loss and facial trauma removed her smile. She ran her index finger lightly across the scar on the right side of his forehead. "Why did you lose so much weight? Does that hurt?"

"I just didn't eat much. I was too busy. And no, honey, it doesn't hurt. It's fine."

"It's still red along the edges. Are they doing anything for that and those awful looking eyes? How'd that happen?"

"They are doing everything that needs to be done, Ang."

"That must have been some fight you were in. Where the hell have you been? And why did they need to get a uniform from me? What happened to the one you left with?"

"All that is behind us, honey. There's no need to get into that."

"Oh! I get it—secrets. OK. Well, take off that gown, and let me see what else happened to you." She winked, reached down, and untied the gown's belt.

Chuckling as he took off the gown and laid it on the bed, he said, "In the Navy, this is called a short-arm inspection."

"Stand at attention for inspection, sailor!" she quipped. "Now turn completely around slowly."

Her eyes became teary when she saw how slim he was and what was left of bruises and scars on his back and buttocks. "Oh, Sal. You weren't just in a fight. You were beaten up real bad. Do you know who did this?"

"Uh, yes, the Navy knows all about it. They took pictures of all that stuff earlier. It's all being taken care of."

"And you can't tell me what happened?"

"It doesn't matter now, honey. I'm putting all that in the past. You need to do that too."

"Oh, I see. I'm never gonna know anything about it. Aye, aye, sailor. No more questions about that. Just tell me one thing. Will it be painful for you to make love to me? Can we? Right now?"

"Painful? Oh, hell no! Get your birthday suit on! We'll have to try to be quiet, so the nurses don't get alarmed."

"That's not going to be easy, Sal," she said saucily.

"Yeah," he laughed, "I know, believe me, it's gonna hurt too, but we're gonna do the best we can. They write down everything in that damn chart, ya know."

They spent the rest of the evening celebrating being together again. They hugged, kissed, made love voraciously, and exhausted themselves repeatedly. Eventually, the sandman visited them. They fell asleep involuntarily after midnight, tangled up in each other's arms and legs.

A noisy bedside phone woke them at 7 a.m., giving them a half-hour warning for breakfast. Angela grabbed a robe, went into the bathroom, and closed the door.

"We gave you an extra hour today, Conte," said the Navy nurse accompanying the Hospital Corpsman that brought breakfast. "Hereafter, it will be 0600. Did you sleep well?" She asked, flashing a smile. The young Corpsman giggled.

"Thank you, ladies! Much appreciated. I slept like a baby," he said, grinning as he sat down at the table.

Angela came out of the bathroom and sat at the table. "Good morning, girls."

"Oh, damn, smell that coffee and the bacon," he said when the Corpsman lifted the cover from their plates and departed the room.

Salvador took a deep breath, "I hope this isn't all a dream. You have no idea how hungry I am."

The nurse laughed, "I'll put on your chart that you had a good night's rest and woke with a good appetite," she said lightheartedly and turned to Angela. "Miss Mirabol, once breakfast is finished, he'll be gone from the room till lunchtime for labs, X-rays, stress test, plus neurology and orthopedic assessments. We're going to make sure he's ship-shape to return to his normal duties."

"I've never been to DC and have wanted to visit the Natural History and Art Museums. Sounds like a good time for me to do that."

"If you plan to be back by 1200, I can schedule two lunches," said the nurse.

"Please do, thank you," said Angela.

"Alright. Also, Miss Mirabol, I noted his schedule is full with Navy officials from 1300 to 1700. A social worker can help you with ideas for things to do during the afternoon if you wish."

Angela topped off their cups from the carafe, "Oh, that's good coffee. Just point me in the right direction to see one of them; thank you."

"No need, Miss Mirabol, I'll just ask a social worker to come to this room at 1300," said the nurse.

"I appreciate that, thank you," said Angela.

"Ma'am, do you know when I'll be discharged?" asked Salvador.

"That, Petty Officer Conte, will depend on what the doctor thinks after he sees the results of your tests and what Captain Patterson has to say."

"I feel great, ma'am. Schedule me out of here at 0800 tomorrow!"

"Sailor, you're just going to have to follow orders and be a compliant patient," the nurse scolded him, partly joking.

He smiled at the nurse devilishly.

"Patience has never been his strong suit," said Angela.

Salvador laughed, "Frankly, I'm actually glad to be here. You all have no idea. I'd rather be home, though. But one thing I can do is follow orders."

"You look tired, Conte," said Patterson after Jefferson and two others with him departed the conference room. It had been a full day of tests, evaluations, and debriefings by Agent Jefferson, Captain Patterson, and a Naval Security Group personal security officer.

"Yes, sir, I am. Being caged like an animal for so long and without much to eat or drink, I have really gotten out of shape."

"I'll come back tomorrow at 0900 and see what the Doc has to say. I talked to him right after lunch, and he thought the preliminary results were optimistic. He thinks, and I'm making no promises now, but he thinks that you could be discharged tomorrow afternoon."

"Sir, I hope so. I can't wait to get back to work and normal married life. I asked Angela to marry me at lunchtime. She said yes, of course."

"Congratulations! Speaking of getting back to work, I have a question for you. As a small token for all you've been through, where would you like to go for duty?"

"When?"

"As soon as we can cut the orders. I talked with your CO at Homestead. You're going to take 30 days leave to recuperate when you're discharged. Doctor's orders. By then, we'll have your orders ready. A Navy doctor will give you a follow-up exam. If he clears you for duty, you'll be able to make arrangements to get your household goods shipped to your new duty station."

"Oh shit! Sorry, sir. I'm just flabbergasted, is all. That's an easy choice for me to make. I have always had Hawaii on my dream sheet. I want to go to Wahiawa, sir! But not in a fleet direct support billet. Not for this tour, anyway. Those guys spend so much time away from home.

But yeah, Hawaii, please, sir. That would be a hell of a great duty station and a terrific place to get married."

Peter J. Azzole

EPILOGUE

Two weeks later, on October 16, 1962, as Salvador and Angela were snorkeling in Key Largo, McGeorge Bundy was briefing President Kennedy about finding the elusive smoking gun in Cuba. An analysis of a U-2 reconnaissance flight over Cuba two days earlier revealed that medium-range ballistic missiles were present.

The President quickly assembled a tight group of high-level military and government officials to determine how to deal with this monumental crisis. That group was termed the "ExComm," the Executive Committee of the National Security Council.

ExComm meeting, White House, Cabinet Room

The ExComm gave the President three options: strictly diplomatic negotiations, a naval blockade of Cuba to preclude the delivery of more weapons to Cuba, and an air attack to destroy the missiles and all the Soviet military sites. JFK chose diplomatic negotiations with a blockade. However, it was called a "quarantine" because a blockade, in international law, is considered an act of war. The quarantine gave them time to negotiate with the Soviet Union to remove all offensive weapons from Cuba. This was the genesis of a hectic and chilling 13-days of political and military confrontation between the United States and the Soviet Union.

At 7 p.m. on October 22, Salvador and Angela were glued to the television in their Key Largo hotel room. A hard lump formed in Salvador's throat as he listened to JFK make a shocking 18-minute radio and television speech from the Oval Office. Angela could not possibly know what this meant to Salvador, nor would she ever.

The President told the American people and the world of

unmistakable evidence of Soviet strategic missiles in Cuba and that the United States could not tolerate this. He announced that he ordered the imposition of a naval quarantine of Cuba. He further explained that he demanded that the Soviets remove their missiles.

Six days later, on October 18, after nearly daily heated exchanges and brinksmanship in diplomatic channels, the leader of the Soviet Union, Nikita Kruschev, signed and released an open letter to JFK, declaring that the Soviet missile systems would be dismantled and removed from Cuba. The crisis was over. The nuclear threat to the United States from Cuba had been eliminated.

The U.S. intelligence agencies continued their heightened focus on Cuba for several months to confirm the removal of the Soviet missile threats, as evidenced by the ExComm meetings on Cuba continuing through March 29, 1963.

Communications Technician (Interpretive) Salvador Conte and Angela Mirabol were married in the Naval Communications Station, Wahiawa, Hawaii base chapel, in the spring of 1963. He was selected for Chief Petty Officer that fall.

In a closed personal ceremony in the office of the Commanding Officer in December 1963, he was awarded the Navy Expeditionary Medal for "duties performed outside the continental United States." The classified version of the justification and citation for this award remained sealed in Washington, DC.

Admiral Kurtz signed a recommendation for an award of higher rank that was being staffed through the Department of the Navy. That recommendation traveled through many offices for years. There was controversy over the proper award owing to the unique situation and sensitivity of Salvador's mission. None of the current awards were fitting. Finally, in 1970, he was one of the first naval personnel to be awarded the Meritorious Service Medal created the previous year. The unclassified description of the nature of his award was notably bland, with the highly classified version remaining sealed."

Salvador never identified any of the Cubans with whom he came in contact, aside from Nilda. His story to the interrogators about her innocence jived with the one she gave them. She suffered extensively at the hands of brutal interrogators, but she never compromised a soul. She was released after several weeks to make room for new prisoners and made her way home to heal. She and all the others who aided Salvador continued their second lives as revolutionists against the Castro regime.

Peter J. Azzole

AUTHOR'S EXPERIENCE IN THE CRISIS

Photo by Peter J. Azzole

NSGA Cape Chiniak, Kodiak Island, AK – Main Building

135

y personal experience with the Cuban Missile Crisis was hardly similar to Salvador Conte's. But I certainly wasn't immune to its impact. During the crisis, I was stationed at Naval Security Group Activity, Cape Chiniak, Kodiak Island, Alaska.

One of the rotating duties of the watch section personnel was to operate the Communications Center that was located at the end of the main building. In a recollection penned years ago, I recalled one of those days in the hectic and chilling "13-days." I'll share an edited version of it.

The Communications Center of Naval Security Group Activity, Cape Chiniak, Alaska, was manned solo during the evening and midnight watches. I don't recall the date or time during this particular eve- or mid-watch, but the ordinarily peaceful routine in the solitude of the communications center was broken. A long string of bells from the teletype on the encrypted circuit with Naval Communications Station, Kodiak, indicated that they had a FLASH precedence message for us, which was rare. Given what we knew about the growing situation in Cuba, it was offputting. I was as anxious as the rest of the crew about the Defense Condition being raised from DefCon-5 to DefCon-3 by the Defense Department worldwide on October 23, 1962. We didn't have as much information as we craved—cable news wasn't conceived yet—but we knew that the U.S. was head-to-head with Kruschev over missiles in Cuba, and a naval quarantine was being imposed. Northern Lights permitting, I usually had a good signal from one of the mainland AM band broadcasting stations during midwatches. I also copied the UPI, Reuters, or AP short-wave teletype circuits for news. These were far richer and more timely sources of information than that received through Navy news summaries. Being out-of-theater for this conflict meant being out of the loop for intelligence reports and advisories related to the Cuban conflict.

Although Cape Chiniak was a long way from Fidel's bastion, we were affected nonetheless. My fall transfer orders to Pensacola had been frozen, as had all Naval Security Group transfers. The Officer in Charge ordered armed security patrols around the operations building and the main complex, as well as dispersal drills, which were akin to abandon-ship.

Oh, those dispersal drills. Each watch section had the pleasure of a trek deep into the southern Kodiak woods for an overnight camp-out with the Officer In Charge. The drill included a simulation of the emergency destruction of all classified documents and equipment, followed by an abandonment of the site far into the woods due to potential invasion by possible captors.

We took only the basics: sleeping bags, C- Rations, coffee grounds, and M-1 carbines without ammunition. An overnight hike in the fall on Kodiak Island is not your basic Indian Summer holiday. It wasn't bitter, but it was cold enough to have been compared by some to a witch's loins or to the hind quarters of a well-digger in Alaska.

When night fell on our campsite, the pine trees groaned from breezes amid a rapid temperature drop. I was introduced to chuckwagon coffee, a handful of grounds thrown into boiling water in an open vessel placed in the center of a wood fire's embers. Picking coffee grounds out of your teeth adds to the thrill of rising victorious over mother nature.

The wonders of chemistry were demonstrated by using self-heating cans of rations. Punching holes in the wide can rim, then pouring water into the holes on the carbide particles in the outer jacket around the contents was designed to heat them. But alas, the centers of the self-heated food were stone cold, as were our tender, spoiled bodies. We quickly committed our hungry hulks to the sleeping bags so that unconsciousness might hasten the coming of the morning and a blessed return to more gentile accommodations. My immediate worry was being stomped on by a deer running through the woods, which delayed drifting off to sleep. At least we knew what it would be like if we really had to do it.

Back to the communications center and the bells. Throughout the U.S. defense system, a general war command post exercise, a paper drill, was being conducted. We had a Russian "fishing ship" sitting south of us in "international waters." All these things mentioned above, in combination, made our geographically isolated souls anxious.

I promptly acknowledged Naval Communication Station Kodiak's raucous bell callup. Pleasantries and chatter were notably absent as the operator merely exchanged encryption setup information, after which we quickly shifted into enciphered traffic mode. Immediately, a FLASH precedence message began revealing itself line by line. My eyes were fixed on the canary yellow paper as I watched each character come to life. Finally, after a gazillion teletype addressees, the classification line revealed itself, "Secret," followed by the subject line, which hardly registered. It was the numbered paragraphs that I was interested in. My patience was rewarded. My stomach turned into butterflies, and my ears became hot when I read the first paragraph of the message: "1. A NUCLEAR ATTACK HAS BEEN LAUNCHED AGAINST THE EAST COAST OF THE UNITED STATES..." It took only moments, but it seemed forever before I regained the composure appropriate for a command post exercise message. The mere thought that it could be a reality was stunning. It made a lasting impression; the potential reality was not lost on me.

Finally, the Soviet missiles were verified to have been removed from Cuba, and the Defense Condition was reduced to normal. I departed for specialty training at the Naval Technical Training Center, Corry Station, Pensacola, FL, just before Christmas 1962.

Suffice it to say the Cuban Missile Crisis has a special meaning for me.

AUTHOR'S NOTES

I would like to thank you, the readers of my work, very much for your interest and support!

Please take a few minutes and go to Amazon, GoodReads, or your favorite online bookstore and give this story a review or rating.

Visit my website or amazon.com for information about other titles of mine:

www.pjazzoleauthor.com

May I also invite you to sign up for my email list to get updates and advance information on upcoming novels? I do not spam the email list, sell it to others, or share it otherwise.

All my very best to you in your reading,

Pete

petej@gate.net

GLOSSARY

Alvarez, Tomas   Fictitious character; auto repair garage owner; CIA contact in Cuba.

Angela Mirabol   A fictitious character; Salvador Conte's girlfriend.

Basilio, Luis, Dr.   Fictitious character; Cuban Director of Health Clinic in the Santa Cruz area.

Bundy, McGeorge (Mac)   Special Assistant to President Kennedy during the missile crisis.

C-Ration   The C-ration, or Type C ration, was a prepared and canned wet combat ration intended to be issued to U.S. military land forces when fresh food (A-ration) or packaged unprepared food (B-ration) prepared in mess halls or field kitchens was not possible or not available.

Callsign   Sequence of alpha-numeric characters that identify the sending or receiving station in telecommunications.

Castaneda, Marco   Fictitious character; revolutionary cell boss for Tomas Alvarez.

Cheche   Fictitious character; bakery owner.

China   Fictitious character; Cheche's wife.

COMINT   Communications Intelligence; the exploitation of communications systems.

Communications Technician (CT)   A Navy rating (specialty), established in 1948. At the time of this story, it was comprised of six career fields identified as branches: A – Administrative, I – Interpretive, O – Communications, M – Maintenance, R – Collection, and T – Technical. CTs were trained in the varied fields of signal intelligence. In 1976, the name of the CT rating was changed to

Cryptologic Technician.

Conte, Salvador   Fictitious protagonist character; US Navy enlisted
                   Communications Technician, Interpretive.

Counter-intelligence (CI)   Information or activities related to the protection of a
                   country against an opposition's total range of intelligence activities.

Cryptology   A broad field of operations that produces communications
                   intelligence (COMINT) and electronic intelligence (ELINT). This
                   involves, but is not limited to, generating strategic and tactical Top
                   Secret intelligence through analysis and exploitation of all forms of
                   electronic signals.

DF   Direction finding/finder; measurement of a single line of magnetic
                   bearing from a known location (DF site); the intersection of lines
                   of bearing from different DF sites determines the location of the
                   signal transmitter.

Dobrynin, Anatoly   Soviet Ambassador to the U.S. during the missile crisis.

Donnelly, Jameson   Fictitious character; Chief Cuban Analysis Group,
                   National Security Agency.

Escalante, Colonel   Fictitious character; Cuban officer, Attaché in the Cuban
                   Embassy in Washington, DC, arrested by the FBI and convicted
                   of crimes.

ETA, ETD   Estimated Time of Arrival/Departure.

Eyes Only   A category of message restricted for viewing only by the person(s)
                   specified.

FKR-1   **English:** The FKR-1 (Frontovaya Krylyatnaya Raketa: Frontline
                   Cruise Missile) was a mobile Ground-Launched Cruise Missile
                   system developed based on the S-2 Sopka version of Mikoyan KS-
                   1 Air-Launched Cruise Missile. This missile was intended to serve
                   as a Nuclear Cruise Missile to support frontline battlefield
                   operations, including anti-ship targets. (Source: Wikimedia
                   Commons)

GMT   Greenwich Mean Time: the meridian of Greenwich, England, is
                   the center of the zero time zone, which is the basis of standard
                   time zones recognized throughout the world.

Groups   In the context of encrypted messages, akin to 'words.' Since there
                   are no words, per se, there are groups of characters, normally all a
                   fixed number of letters, e.g., five-letter groups.

HF Band   High frequency (HF) is the international designation for the range

141

of radiofrequency electromagnetic waves (radio waves) between 3 and 30 megahertz (MHz). HF wavelengths range from ten to one hundred meters.

HFDF   High frequency (aka shortwave) direction finding/finder.

HUMINT   Human Intelligence; information obtained from human sources (spy, interrogation, etc.).

Ibarra-Alvarez, Dalita   Fictitious character; wife of Tomas Alvarez.

Jefferson, Marvin   Fictitious character; CIA special operations manager.

Kennedy, Robert   Attorney General of the U.S. during the missile crisis.

Koskov, Colonel   Fictitious character; commander of a Soviet missile base in Cuba.

Kurtz, Admiral   Rear Admiral Thomas R., Commander, Naval Security Group Command from July 1961 to August 1963.

Laline   Fictitious character; wife of Cuban sugar cane farmer Raúl.

Luna-M   The 9K52 Luna-M, NATO reporting name FROG-7 is a Soviet short-range artillery rocket system that fires unguided and spin-stabilized 9M21 rockets. Initially developed in the 1960s to provide divisional artillery support using tactical nuclear weapons but was gradually modified for conventional use.

McCone, John   Director of Central Intelligence during the missile crisis.

Melnikov, Molot, Major   Fictitious character; Soviet KGB Officer in Cuba.

Mirabol, Angela   Fictitious character; Salvador Conte's girlfriend.

National Security Agency (NSA)   U.S. agency under the Secretary of Defense responsible for signal intelligence operations worldwide.

Naval Security Group (OP-20-G)   Navy organization under the Office of Chief of Naval Operations (OPNAV), 20th Division, the Office of Naval Communications, G Section/Communications Security; the unclassified title of the U.S. Navy's signals intelligence and cryptanalysis headquarters during World War II. It was located on the top floor of the Main Navy Building, Constitution Avenue, Washington, DC, until it moved to 3801 Nebraska Avenue, NW, DC, in February 1943.

Naval Security Group Activity   An operations site under the Naval Security Group Command.

Nilda   Fictitious character; Salvador's driver (toward NAS Guantanamo)

One-time-pad	An encryption technique that cannot be cracked but requires the use of a one-time pre-shared key the same size as, or longer than, the message being sent. In this technique, the plaintext is paired with a random secret key (also referred to as a one-time pad). Then, each bit or character of the plaintext is encrypted by combining it with the corresponding bit or character from the pad using modular addition. If the key is truly random, is at least as long as the plaintext, is never reused in whole or in part, and is kept completely secret, then the resulting ciphertext will be impossible to decrypt.
OP-20-G	Office of Chief of Naval Operations (OPNAV), 20th Division, the Office of Naval Communications, G Section/Communications Security; the unclassified title of the U.S. Navy's signals intelligence and cryptanalysis headquarters during World War II. It was located on the top floor of the Main Navy Building, Constitution Avenue, Washington, DC, until it moved to 3801 Nebraska Avenue, NW, DC, in February 1943.
Operation Cymbal Beat	A fictitious operation to put a voice intercept operator into Cuba.
Operation MONGOOSE	The Cuban Project, also known as Operation MONGOOSE, was an extensive campaign of terrorist attacks against civilians, and covert operations, carried out by the U.S. Central Intelligence Agency in Cuba. It was officially authorized on November 30, 1961, by President John F. Kennedy. The operation was run out of a major secret United States covert operations, and intelligence gathering station established a year earlier in Miami, Florida. (Source: excerpted from Wikipedia)
Patterson, Daniel, Captain	Fictitious character; Head, Ops. Dept., OP-20-G.
Petty Officer	A Navy non-commissioned officer. Seniority is designed by classes. Petty Officer First Class, as is Salvador Conte. It is the senior enlisted rank below Chief Petty Officer.
Raúl	Fictitious character; Cuban sugar cane farmer.
RI	(Radio Intercept) The term for intercepting radio communications between two entities without their knowledge.
Rusk, Dean	Secretary of State during the missile crisis.
Salvador Conte	Fictitious character, the protagonist
Scuttlebutt	A common Navy slang meaning gossip, idle chatter.
SEAL	The United States Navy Sea, Air, and Land (SEAL) Teams,

commonly known as Navy SEALs, are the U.S. Navy's primary special operations force. Among the SEALs' main functions are conducting small-unit special operation missions in maritime, jungle, urban, arctic, mountainous, and desert environments.

Sergio   Salvador Conte's covername in Cuba.

Ship's Company   Those personnel permanently assigned to a ship or shore station.

Skinny   Navy slang for information.

Dalita Ibarra-Alvarez   Fictitious character; wife of Tomas Alvarez.

Sorensen, Theodore   Special Counsel to President Kennedy during the missile crisis.

TAD   Temporary Additional Duty.

Tomas Alvarez   Fictitious character; auto repair garage owner; CIA contact in Cuba.

Transceiver   Radio equipment designed to both transmit and receive.

Travkin, Lieutenant   Fictitious character; KGB officer assigned to a Soviet missile base.

UHF (Ultra High Frequency)   is the ITU designation for radio frequencies in the range between 300 megahertz (MHz) and 3 gigahertz (GHz). UHF radio waves propagate mainly by line of sight; they are blocked by hills and large buildings, although the transmission through building walls is strong enough for indoor reception.

Very Well   U.S. Navy phrase used by a senior to acknowledge a statement, advisory, or report from a junior.

VHF (Very High Frequency)   is the range of radio frequency electromagnetic waves (radio waves) from 30 to 300 megahertz (MHz). VHF radio waves propagate mainly by line-of-sight, so they are blocked by hills and mountains, although due to refraction, they can travel somewhat beyond the visual horizon out to about 160 km (100 miles).

Voronin, Arseny   Fictitious character; KGB Officer in the Soviet Consulate in San Francisco who surrendered for asylum.

***

ABOUT THE AUTHOR

Peter J. Azzole is a retired U.S. Navy Officer who served for 20 years of active duty as a cryptology specialist. His Navy career encompassed several aspects of communications intelligence abroad, afloat, and in the United States. After retirement from the Navy, he worked in the Defense, Commercial Airline, and Healthcare industries.

Peter currently resides in New Bern, NC.

Made in the USA
Middletown, DE
03 November 2022

14038945R00104